Table of

CW00547933

The Curious Case of the Vanishing Victims

A Justin Case Adventure Trilogy
Justin Case Mystery Series:
Our First Case
by
James D. A. Terry

Story Told by: Justin Case

Copyright © 2019 James D. A. Terry
All rights reserved. First Printing: 2019. The editorial arrangement, analysis, and professional commentary are subject to this copyright notice. No portion of this book may be copied, retransmitted, reposted, duplicated, or otherwise used without the express written approval of the author, except by reviewers who may quote brief excerpts in connection with a review.
United States laws and regulations are public domain and not subject to copyright. Any unauthorized copying, reproduction, translation, or distribution of any part of this material without permission by the author is prohibited and against the law.
Disclaimer and Terms of Use: This is a work of fiction. Names, characters, businesses, places, events and incidents are either the products of the author's imagination or used in a fictitious manner. Any resemblance to actual persons, living or dead or actual events is purely coincidental.
ISBN- 9798223681274 Paperback

PRAISE FOR THE JUSTIN CASE MYSTERIES

Congratulations on a wonderful and most enjoyable book. Thanks for letting me read your book.

The Curious Case of the Vanishing Victims is a rare treat: fresh, original and funny. A new twist on the Repo Man, Justin Case is not your average investigator. Buy it! Now!

Alan Bradley, New York Times bestselling author of the Flavia de Luce mysteries. And a new one coming soon!

Dive into the captivating world of intrigue and amateur sleuthing with James D. A. Terry's masterful mystery, THE CURIOUS CASE of the VANISHING VICTIMS. With a delightful blend of charm and humor, the author's skillful uses of aptronyms are sure to have you laughing out loud. Yet, beyond the laughter, lies the true brilliance of the story—a sincere commitment to unraveling a perplexing case. For those who relish unearthing mysteries alongside endearing characters, this book will hold you spellbound from the very first page to the closing word. Your anticipation will soar as you eagerly await the unfolding of this exceptional narrative journey.

Ang Pompano, Agatha nominated author

Written for both teens and adults, *The Curious Case of the Vanishing Victims*, by James D. A. Terry, is a fun romp. Serious at times, whimsical at others, this light-hearted mystery—sprinkled with mythological and historical references—offers quirky characters, puzzling plots (there are three separate stories), and satisfying conclusions. A sure bet for readers looking for something fanciful.

Carol Pouliot, author of **The Blackwell and Watson Time-Travel Mysteries**

The Curious Case of the Vanishing Victims is a lively ride with an appealing and relatable main character. It keeps readers guessing right to the unexpected and thought-provoking end; a traditional mystery with a twist and some extra heart and soul.

Kathleen Marple Kalb, author of the **Ella Shane and Old Stuff Mysteries** and (as **Nikki Knight**), author of **WRONG POISON,** Vermont Radio Mysteries Derringer Finalist. Vice President, Short Mystery Fiction Society

I loved The Curious Case of the Vanishing Victims by James Terry. It is funny and quirky, but it has a resonance of reality, or some altered version of one that makes you want to keep turning the pages to find out what happens next. Justin Case, the self-deprecating narrator and would-be hero is a very interesting protagonist who you grow to like, despite his many flaws.

I highly recommend The Curious Case of the Vanishing Victims for anyone who likes humour with their murder and international intrigue in their mystery. Can't wait for the rest of this series.

Mike Martin, Author of the Award-Winning and Best-Selling **Sgt. Windflower Mystery series.**

ACKNOWLEDGEMENTS

Writing a book is harder than I thought and more rewarding than I ever could have imagined.

I offer a truly heartfelt thank you to my wife, Christine, for patiently reading and rereading the seemingly endless drafts, wise advice and unwavering support. I couldn't have done it without you.

Thank you to Susan (Susi) Castro, Kathy Lee, and Una Tiers, three consummate professionals, for their diligent efforts in editing my work. You made this book eminently more readable than it otherwise might have been.

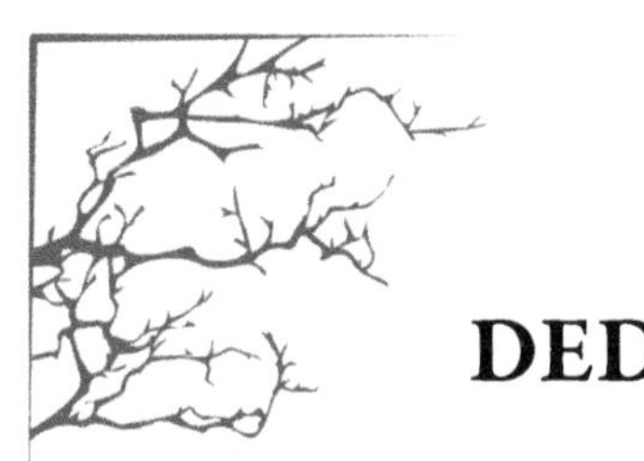

DEDICATION

This book is dedicated to my brothers from other mothers.
Some people don't believe in heroes. But they haven't met my brothers from other mothers.

A brother from another mother is a blessing, a friend who becomes the family you choose for yourself, and a bond that lasts forever.
He's seen you at your best and your worst and still accepts you for who you are.
Only a brother can love like a father, annoy like a sister, care like a mother and support like a friend.
Brotherhood means I will always come for you no matter the cost.
Greater Love has no one than this that he lay down his life for his friends. - **John 15:13 NIV**

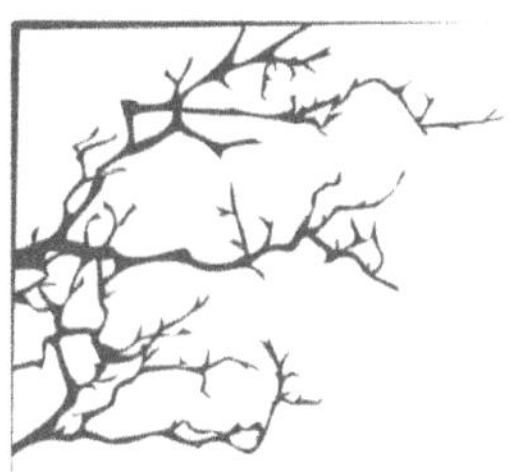

PROLOGUE

Every culture identifies with unique traditions and mythologies. Myths serve a profound role in cultures and traditions around the world, anchoring us to a sense of history and meaning through allegorical storytelling. In Scotland, for instance, the highland people have the legend of the Banshee. The indigenous tribes of Australia share tales of the Warrigal. In the Americas, the original northern inhabitants, the Algonquians, tell their story of the legendary Wendigo, the "malevolent spirit of lonely places.

The ancient North American legend depicts the monster as the by-product of cannibalism or dark magic. With each feed, the Wendigo grows bigger and stronger and needs a bigger meal to fill it. In some myth variations, people can also become a Wendigo after merely coming into contact with it or the creature could possess them in a dream. After it takes control of its host, the beast assumes the identity of the person.

Like many urban legends of monsters and cryptids, there is a conspicuous lack of concrete proof of its existence beyond second-hand accounts and witness testimonies.

The wendigo as a concept, can apply to any person, idea, or movement infected by a corrosive drive toward self-aggrandizing greed and excessive consumption, traits that sow disharmony and destruction if left unchecked. In addition to characterizing individual people who exhibit destructive tendencies, the wendigo can also describe movements and events with similarly negative effects. According to Professor Chris Schedler, the idea of the wendigo represents "consuming forms of exclusion and assimilation" through which groups dominate other groups.

It can serve as a metaphor explaining any pattern of domination by which groups subjugate and dominate or violently destroy and displace. Wendigos are agents of "social cannibalism" who know "no provincial or national borders; all human cultures have been visited by shape-shifting wendigos. Their visitations speak to the inseparability of human experience. National identity is irrelevant to this borderless horror. An expression of a dark aspect of human nature: the drive toward greed, consumption, and disregard for other life in the pursuit of self-aggrandizement.

In the 1987 movie Wall Street, Gordon Gekko proclaims that "...greed—for the lack of a better word—is good."

The reality is that we are all susceptible to greed. We are compelled to satisfy our desires with the least possible expenditure of effort, often at the expense of others.

My name is Case... Justin Case, termination agent subcontracted by the Tin Can Communications Company (TCC). My mission, should I accept it, is to repossess equipment belonging to the TCC and I have tales to tell so incredible that I'm not certain even I believe them.

A Legend Awakened a Legacy Revealed

The first of three adventures linked by a common thread in the trilogy of Chasing the Wendigo as told by

Justin Case

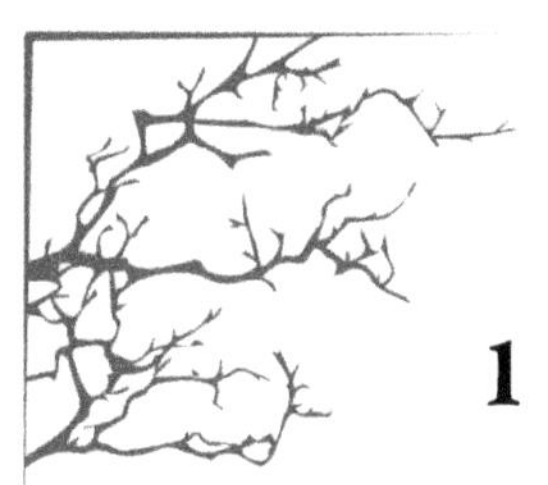

1 sleepy hollow, it ain't

Thunderheads looming on the horizon were a portent of the approaching storm. My umbrella and rain gear in the backseat I checked in with my handler. After receiving my instructions I set out to roam the county roads in my quest for my next designated task.

My name is Case; Justin Case, Termination Agent for the Tin Can Communications Company. The TCC Co. has a virtual monopoly on the telephone service and rental of telephones in the province. My mission, should I accept it, is to recover telephones abandoned by their lessee or for breach of the lease agreement by the lessee, for the telephone company. I'd like to say that I had been carefully selected for this position from a long list of highly trained professionals because of my particular skill set but; I'd be lying.

It's 1970; a new word has entered the Canadian vocabulary: stagflation, the combination of a stagnant economy and a rising cost of living. After decades of economic growth, those of us just out of school struggle to find our first jobs. I had been searching for my first J.O.B. (Just Over Broke or Just Obey your Boss).

Nicholas, Nick to his friends, and Nathanial, or Nat but we call him Nack, Tchotchke, twenty-year-old twins of Italian and Nordic descent with chestnut brown hair and brown-green eyes, had landed jobs as a string installer (lineman), and tin can (telephone) installer respectively for the Tin Can Communications Company.

Lawson D. Woods, a sandy-haired, lean; mean fighting machine, always ready to lend a hand had also landed a job as a tin can installer with the Tin Can Communications Company.

The Bear, is, well, built like a bear. A logistician with a reserved yet willful personality, and a rational outlook on life, had also landed a job as a tin can installer with the TCC Company.

Hugo First, an auburn-haired casanova of the group possessing extraordinary physical abilities, a receding hairline and freckles with a barely visible scar where someone had tried to decapitate him on a snowmobile trail, but that's a story for another day, is a pile-it for Clickety-Clack Railway; he piles it here and piles it there.

Moose, a purveyor of obscure facts, weighing in at 98 pounds soaking wet and whose glasses seemed to be perpetually slipping down his nose, is a bean counter for the company that makes telephone equipment. He is reliable, practical, grounded, and logical even in the most stressful situations.

Me? Well, I'm a little overweight and wear glasses as thick as Coke bottle bottoms. I wish I could lose weight as easily as I lose my key, pen, temper, and even my mind. You might think I'm introverted but let's just say I prefer my own company shall we? They say still waters run deep. My alone time is sometimes for your safety. I admit to a mild case of OCD and some say I tend to be judgemental but I like things done properly and logically.

So, I applied to the TCC Co. but was told they weren't hiring any more staff; at this time. However, after unrelenting persistence, I was finally offered a subcontracting job of equipment recovery at a princely rate of 11 cents per mile and a set amount per phone.

The rough grey water of the bay looked cold and angry as the howling wind whipped the waves into a frenzy of white caps. A sudden gust of wind walloped my car as if an unseen hand had delivered a body blow as I fought to maintain control of my vehicle. My tires made a loud thrumming sound on the metal grid of the swing bridge wobbling uncontrollably like the wheels of my childhood go-kart. Leaving the bridge behind me, I travelled deeper into the county on my quest.

My first destination was an upstairs apartment in the bustling village of Farshore, where I met with a certain amount of angry resistance from the tenant. "Who're you and waddya want?" he muttered through the half-open door.

My sense of smell was immediately assaulted by the fetid odour emanating through the narrow opening. Without thinking, I tried to hold my breath to avoid inhaling the invisible clouds of who knows what filling the apartment and spilling out into the corridor. I could feel them enveloping me. I didn't want to open my mouth to speak but managed to mutter, "Case; Justin Case,

Termination Agent for the Tin Can Communications Company" I spluttered; as I was forced to inhale. "I'm here to retrieve the company's equipment," I replied in my most businesslike manner.

"I need it. You have no right to take it." The surly, unshaven lodger shouted in angry protest.

Believe me, I don't want to touch it or even enter your apartment. I thought but said, "I've been authorized to remove the company's equipment due to lack of payment." I raised the TCC requisition for him to see. He squinted in the murky atmosphere of the dimly lit hallway.

"But, it came with the apartment." Whined the barefooted occupant, clad in a sleeveless undershirt displaying a myriad of unknown stains and brandishing a butcher knife.

"You were the sole applicant in the rental contract you signed with the TCC. You agreed to make monthly payments for the use of the rented equipment and have failed to make the last three months' payments. You have left the TCC no choice but to cut off your service." A poor choice of words in light of the lethal weapon he wielded. Glancing at the implement of my potential grizzly end I shuddered as I noticed what appeared to be remnants of his previous victims still on the blade.

He wasn't giving up easily. His hand holding the knife twitched fretfully as images of my imminent demise skittered through my imagination. I most definitely did *not* want to end up face-down in this squalid dump. "I have a child. What about emergencies? Doesn't anybody care about that?" he groused.

"The equipment is of no use to you anyway because your service has been cut off. I'm afraid I have no other choice than to take it" again that poor turn of phrase given the circumstances.

The sorry-looking specimen with a hand-rolled cigarette dangling from his drooping mouth stepped back a half step to allow me just enough space to enter. The pong of sweat, beer and stale tobacco overwhelmed my senses as I cautiously stepped through the narrow space afforded me. I got no help from the hapless and indifferent occupant as I searched the apartment for equipment to be seized. Lifting a pile of filthy clothing from an end table with my screwdriver, knocking over an empty beer can and scattering cigarette butts on the floor I located a black, rotary dial desk handset.

Unenthusiastically I made my way to the kitchen. Each foot made a vile sticking sound with every step. Every flat surface was piled with dirty dishes and the stench of decay filled the room. I discovered a grease-coated wall-mounted beige rotary device which I hastily yet gingerly removed.

My task was completed and I looked around but saw no sign of the tenant I thought, *somewhere out there is a tree tirelessly producing oxygen so you can breathe. I think you owe it an apology.* But instead called out, "Thank you." and quickly exited the apartment.

The billowing storm clouds had closed in making it so dark the street lights had come on. Placing the gear in the trunk of my car I meticulously wiped my face, hands, and arms with a disinfectant cloth, wishing I could shower, then checked my list for the next location. The requisition told me it was situated in the farthest reaches of the county on the Great Lake's shore. A note told me the property was abandoned and I would need to stop in at the municipal office to obtain a key.

Like a threatening augury of the approaching storm, the first sprinkles of rain dotted the pavement as I pulled into the municipal office parking lot. Far-off rumbles of thunder could be heard. Light glowed from every window giving a deceptive appearance of welcoming.

What should have been a brief stop became a bureaucratic tangle of red tape. I was greeted by a very officious and stern, Mrs. Eileen Wright, her head and shoulders just visible above the counter. She stood about five foot two, weighed in at about ninety-eight pounds soaking wet, with a head of nicotine-stained hair having the appearance of rusty steel wool. Her icy stare from cold, black eyes could cause the blood of the most stalwart of men to run cold with trepidation. Mine was, apparently, an unusual request according to Mrs. Wright, as she assailed me, "Name and state your business."

"Ju...Justin C...Case, termination agent, subcontracted by the Tin Can Communications Company to recover equipment belonging to them from the house at fire number 1758 Sleepy Hollow Lane. The residence is described as abandoned so I'll need the key." I stammered showing her my requisition.

Her eyebrow arched suspiciously. "I never heard of such a thing. Why would we allow you access and what right do you have to take the equipment?" she snarled.

I could see this was going to be a tough nut to crack. "The bill for the rental of the phones has not been paid and the customer's contract has expired. The company would simply like to recover their property." I replied.

"There's nothing simple about it. This is a very unusual request I must say." With that, she gave me a withering look of evident contempt and reached beneath the counter withdrawing a large red-covered record book. Opening it to an empty page she shoved the open book across the counter instructing me to, "Place the date here." indicating with her nicotine-stained finger. "Print your full name where it says 'print name' and sign beside it. Write down your address and phone number here, where it says 'contact details'. Insert the description of the property you wish to visit and why, below.

Read this document accepting full responsibility and liability then sign and date it here." Again she pointed to a line at the bottom of page three.

I felt like I was buying the house not merely gaining access to remove a few communication devices.

"What if I find damage that I was not responsible for?"

She didn't answer merely scowled as she handed me the key with apparent reluctance glaring at me as I turned to leave.

I checked the fire number and plotted my route to 1758, started the engine, switched on the headlights and was off to the next target.

Leaving the lighted streets of the village behind me I plunged into the wide, yawning black infinity in every direction. The sensation of depth beyond the gleam of my headlights was overwhelming. Strong, angry winds pummelled my car. My sense of speed was distorted due to the lack of peripheral cues like fence posts or trees and turns in the road seemed to appear without warning making them more difficult to negotiate. It seemed to take forever to reach my destination. It was hard to make good time when I had to slow down and sometimes come to a complete stop to scan fire numbers, mailboxes and road signs with my flashlight to get my bearings.

Then, just as I was about to give up, my headlights illuminated the sign that read, Sleepy Hollow Lane. The pavement was broken up and weeds were beginning to reclaim the land as they grew up through the cracks. My car jolted and shuddered as I negotiated the old road.

At last, I came to the end of the road and the last fire number was almost utterly obscured beneath a wild and tangled undergrowth of vines, scrub cedar trees and aptly named buckthorn bushes. The wind howled around me as I left the security of my vehicle. Headlamp in place on my forehead I struggled to tug the clinging vegetation from the small plaque displaying the number. The needle-sharp points of the thorns of the buckthorn tore at my skin as if to prevent me from reaching my goal. Finally, in the light from my headlamp there, it was 1758, the number I sought. This was the place.

Getting back behind the wheel of the Mustang I turned into the rutted and overgrown drive. Passing through a rust-encrusted wrought iron gate and under the huge low hanging branches of an ancient oak tree the headlights swept across the corner of what appeared in the gloom to be a marble portico. Suddenly, a brilliant flash of lightning split the sky unexpectedly, illuminating a massive stone edifice rising from the mist before me like a colossal obelisk. I noticed in that flash that all the windows were barred. *Was that to keep intruders out or keep something in?* I wondered as I brought the Mustang to an abrupt halt at the base of the main entrance I hesitated before stepping from the car, unsure of whether or not to go in or just turn around and head for home.

I heard the subtle bass rumbling and felt the forewarning vibrations in the air around me but before I could raise my hands to cover my ears there was a thunderous explosion erupting into an enormous crack and rumble of thunder that shook the ground. The first fat drop of rain hit the windshield splattering like an overfilled water balloon.

I dove for the car just in time to avoid being soaked to the skin by the torrent of rain that quickly followed. Thinking to myself that retreat was the better part of valour I decided to go home and return in the daylight when the weather was better and I could explore the spooky old pile.

Starting my engine I began to back down the drive but just as I drew near to the enormous oak a dazzling bolt of lightning struck the tree severing one of its massive limbs just missing the Mustang's trunk as it fell. I slammed on the brakes and the car skidded to a halt within inches of impact. I was trapped.

I waited as the adrenaline rush subsided then weighed my limited options. I could attempt to move the gigantic branch by pushing it with the car but that would mean damage to my prized possession, spend the night there or ride out the storm and re-evaluate my options.

The first thing to do was to get out from under the trees so I pulled up in front of the steps to the front door of the dark and quietly brooding mansion and turned off the engine. Fortunately, the afternoon was warm and the night was not going to be cold so I sat in quiet contemplation as the storm raged around me.

It wasn't long before the storm's fury settled down enough for me to get out of the car and climb the three, slick from rain, granite steps, glistening in the light from my flashlight to the imposing oak double doors. Rummaging in my pocket I got hold of the key and tried to insert it into the ancient lock. It was no use the key would simply not go into the lock. *That's odd. I wonder if that old battleaxe gave me the wrong key after all the administrative claptrap. I'll give her a piece of my mind when I get back.* I thought to myself with false bravado.

Grasping the tarnished solid bronze Georgian door handle, it felt cold in my hand, I twisted and it turned easily. To my surprise, it was unlocked. The great door creaked in annoyance at being disturbed. The absence of any light within seemed so complete and so utterly dense that the beam from my headlamp seemed to be absorbed before revealing any details of the inner space before me. I was reminded of a song by Simon and Garfunkel, "The Sounds of Silence". I could hear the lyrics, "Hello darkness my old friend, I've come to talk with you again". I did a quick sweep with my more powerful handheld flashlight for any unwelcome surprises like dinner plate size spiders before stepping apprehensively into the entrance hall.

Closing the door against the tumult outside and extinguishing my light I stood motionless listening for any evidence of life in the darkness such as footsteps, breathing, snoring or suchlike. The house was supposed to be abandoned and contained three phone sets with long-since expired contracts. It seems that telephone recovery is not a company priority. Despite that, I waited and listened, understanding the great gulf between what you think you know and reality. The house-made so much noise I was having trouble discerning what was ambient and what might be signs of life. All the cracking, creaking and groaning was nothing that couldn't be explained by the wind and the contraction of ancient wood and plaster. Suddenly the old house's sounds were drowned out by a crescendo of the loudest roar of thunder I had ever heard. The rumbling reverberated throughout the old house.

Then, there came an incongruous tapping. *It must be something loose disturbed by the wind.*

Inhaling deeply to calm my nerves I detected the indelible pong of wood smoke and nicotine that the old house had been marinated in over its long life. Switching my light back on I admired the wide plank hand planed and hand-finished oak floor that groaned and creaked under my weight; above me hung a very heavy twelve light solid bronze hanging chandelier. Under the chandelier sat the only furnishing, a forty-two-inch diameter Georgian centre table with ebony and maple inlay, its surface scarred and misshapen by years of neglect and dampness. There were large archways to my left and right, a mahogany staircase about twenty feet from where I stood and beyond that more rooms, probably the servants' quarters and kitchen.

Why was it so profoundly dark? Turning to my left I entered a cavernous room. The focal point of the empty room was a sophisticated Georgian fireplace of black Kilkenny marble with large deeply carved Irish corbels. Positioned as if to take advantage of the heat from the fireplace sat two dilapidated lawn chairs encircled by empty wine bottles and assorted detritus. Then I noticed the reason the darkness was so intense. The floor-to-ceiling windows facing the lake were shuttered but even so, the light should have leaked around the edges. Moving closer to a window I discovered that the windows were not only shuttered but had also been tightly boarded up into the bargain. I then swept the entire room with my flashlight. On the wall opposite the windows was a floor-to-ceiling ornately carved mahogany bookcase still filled with books.

As the light played over the shelves I noticed that there were gaps between the books as if there had been miscellaneous items and knick-knacks at various intervals that had been removed. Stepping closer I surveyed the books. Many of the tomes looked very old. *Did somebody read all of these or were they just for show? I wonder why no one has taken the books. They're going to get musty and rot if someone doesn't look after them.*

Hmm, I recognize some of these titles. Maybe I should pick a few to read. I muttered to myself as I pulled out a fusty old copy of Treasure Island and opened the cover to read, Robert Louis Stevenson, London: Cassel, 1883. Replacing it I pulled out the next book, The Adventures of Huckleberry Finn, Mark Twain, 1885, Charles L. Webster and signed by Mark Twain, himself. Scanning the shelves I recognized other notable works such as Atlas Shrugged, The Grapes of Wrath and others.

A library fit for a stately home. Well, it's time I was getting to work. I said to myself, walking back to the foyer and crossing the hall to enter the library. The bright light of my torch illuminated a room lined with more, floor-to-ceiling ornately carved mahogany bookshelves, matching the ones in the other room, and an archway to my left opened into what I presumed to be the dining room. Again I saw books leaning askew randomly as if things had been removed from between them.

Taking a quick look around I spotted wear marks on the wide planks from years of a chair rolling back and forth behind a desk and on the floor where a desk would have been I saw a cigar box. Cautiously I raised the lid and there, concealed inside the box lay a fragile and yellowed, with age, copy of Picturesque Prince Edward County by Himmler Renell, 1890 open to page 42, "A Cask of Gold" by H. C. Widdowfield. I absently glanced at the contents and instantly became intrigued.

Imagine finding a cask of lost gold. I thought. I've always been an inquisitive person when something piqued my interest I was like a dog with a bone. I couldn't let it go until I had solved whatever particular riddle had intrigued me.

Oft times I looked to my brothers from other mothers and their unique talents to reach a satisfactory conclusion.

My go-to guy and closest friend, Lawson D. Woods is a sandy-haired and blue-eyed five foot-seven lean mean fighting machine with an outgoing personality and a take-charge attitude always ready to lend a hand.

Nicholas and Nack Tchotchke are steady, easy-going guys always ready with a word of encouragement.

The Romeo in the group, Hugo First, possessed outstanding athletic ability and hand-eye coordination.

Rounding out our six-pack is our fount of facts, appearing as if he would weigh in at 98 pounds soaking wet, a bespectacled Moose.

Heaven only knows why such a diversely talented band of brothers, accepted me but they did and I'll be forever grateful.

Noticing the sound and fury of the storm had abated for the moment; I decided that since I had not found the phone sets listed on the ground floor yet, my only option was to search the rest of this floor. I left the library and entered the foyer once more. I glanced at the elongated shadow on the wall cast by the chandelier and thought I noticed movement. Was the room swaying or was it my imagination? I was taken aback to detect an almost imperceptible oscillation to and fro of the chandelier. I closed my eyes and tried to sense any movement of air on my face. If I felt anything it came from in front of me in the direction of the kitchen. I would try to locate the source of the draft and maybe I'd find the missing phone sets.

Walking towards the back of the house I passed the foot of the grand staircase and in a recess under the stairs was a small door. My guess was the door opened onto stairs leading down to the basement. I was ***not*** going down those stairs.

Opposite the small door under the stairs was another door into the dining room.

The unpleasant smell of rancid cooking odours and the revolting sight of thousands of dead flies everywhere turned my stomach and I realized I hadn't had lunch and was now missing supper. Scanning the kitchen in search of a phone, I saw two doors, one opened into a small, windowless servants' bedroom containing a single folding steel cot and a night table. The other opened to the pantry and servants' entrance.

The single window had been raised about three inches allowing a breeze to flow through. "But surely this slight breeze was not enough to swing such a heavy chandelier, was it?

Where were the phones and what was up with that key?" I thought to myself.

The storm was easing off; it was time to leave if I could. I retraced my steps toward the front of the old house but as I passed under the chandelier I couldn't resist glancing upward and sure enough, it was gently swinging ever so slightly. Could something or someone on the floor above be causing the uncanny motion?

Knowing I wouldn't be able to rest until I had assured myself that I had searched the old house thoroughly, exhausting all possibilities. Apprehensively I climbed the decrepit old staircase and as I climbed I became increasingly aware of a putrid stench that increased in intensity as I ascended. The cacophony of creaking and cracking noises as I climbed was deafening in the hushed darkness so I began placing my feet tight to the inside and outside of the treads where the support was strongest and helped to dampen the sound.

There were four doors off the landing. Peering into the open door of the first bedroom on my left I saw only an old and very basic steel bed, nightstand and a single wooden chair. Continuing along the hall the following two bedrooms were identically furnished. The putrid pong was overwhelming as I reached the last door at the front of the house. This was the room directly over the entranceway. I stood with my hand poised on the knob of the closed door afraid of what horror might await me on the other side. A draft from within rattled the door. Listening intently, as if my life depended on it, I could just make out a slow rhythmical sound like that of someone rocking.

I should have left while I had the chance. Should I make a hasty exit now? Images of all manner of evil lurking behind the door flashed through my mind. My hand was on the handle and as I began to slowly turn it I discovered it was locked. The clicking sound of the handle echoed in the room beyond and I was sure it had alerted whatever or whoever waited behind the door. I called out, "Hello. Is there someone in there?"

"Tap, tap, tap;" came the response.

Startled I said, "My name is Case; Justin Case. Do you need help?" There was no reply. I tried the knob once more. It was locked from the inside. I could just make out barely audible yet monotonously repetitive sounds of movement from within.

I needed to get in there. I knelt to look through the keyhole but something blocked the light. I saw tiny white fibres clinging to the edges of the keyhole and detected a very faint whiff of something burnt. The key must still be in the lock.

I took out the map I always carried in my tool bag and unfolded it. I slipped it under the door and then gently pushed my screwdriver into the keyhole dislodging the key. It landed with a clatter on my map. Whoever or whatever lurked behind the door must certainly be alerted now.

Withdrawing the map and picking up the key I peered through the keyhole and as I did so I got a faint, very faint whiff of something burnt. It was futile; I could see nothing in the inky darkness of the room.

I quickly unlocked the door and with one rapid motion I pushed the door wide holding my flashlight at the ready to use as a weapon I swept the room for any threat. Casting the powerful beam about the room as swiftly as possible my gaze fell upon the sole furnishing of the room, a heavy solid oak Victorian-style rocking chair. Something sat motionless shrouded in a sheet as the chair rocked slowly back and forth, back and forth. I found it impossible to take my eyes off the ghastly shape. I was rooted to the spot in macabre fascination as my blood ran cold.

The soft sound of wood on wood and the creek of ancient wooden joints made the hair on the back of my neck stand to attention. It was as if a ghostly presence occupied the old rocker.

It was then I noticed, the shutters were wide open and the window was up about six inches allowing a strong draught blowing off the lake to flow through the room, not to mention the driving rain. A large puddle had formed on the floor below the window and perched on the sill was a large, midnight-black raven eyeing me ominously. "Murdrum" It croaked then disappeared through the open window into the storm.

'Was I hallucinating? Did that bird just talk? What next? Could this day get any weirder?' I thought as I drew near the chair dreading what I would find. Just then the storm unleashed its full fury as a powerful gust of wind struck the old house with tremendous force. A violent blast of wind raged through the open window sending the chair and its passenger careening forward. The figure's head lolled gruesomely in the violently pitching chair. "It was getting up!" I involuntarily took two steps back with one hand groping for the door behind me.

Then the shroud slid down revealing a hideous desiccated form. The expression on the face of the decomposing corpse was one of shock and horror.

Droplets of the sweat of fear broke out on my forehead and I felt nausea rising from the pit of my stomach.

The cadaver remained fixed and upright in the chair. "How was that possible?" I asked myself and then in the beam of my flashlight, I saw the tape binding the wrists and ankles. "This was murder!"

My thoughts ran riot, "It's too late for a doctor. I need to inform the police. I mustn't touch anything. I should shut the window. That puddle will damage the beautiful oak floor. Who was this person and what happened to them? No time to mop up the water on the floor." My jumbled thoughts tumbled frantically. "Gotta get outta here!" was my final thought as I beat a hasty retreat.

Before I realized it I had descended the stairs to the entry hall where I was greeted by loud scratching noises that echoed through the old house emanating from what I believed to be the cellar door. "Whatever that is I don't want to meet it." I thought to myself. I heaved open the heavy oak door to make good my escape but just as I was closing the door I thought I heard the scrabbling of claws on the hardwood floor."It's coming after me!"

The storm had exhausted its wrath. The shimmering cold blue-white light of the full moon revealed a semi-circular driveway and I laughed nervously out loud while mentally kicking myself. "I could have simply driven out and been home warm, dry and comfortable. I still didn't get what I came for and now I've got to get to the nearest police station as quickly as possible; if nothing else stands in my way." I thought to myself, looking over my shoulder as I raced to my car as if my life depended on it. I slid quickly behind the wheel, stealing a look into the back seat hoping to find it empty, then shutting and locking the door behind me. Fumbling nervously with the keys and almost dropping them in my panic I inserted the ignition key and turned it, there was no sound. I tried it again, but nothing. Then I realized that in the chaos I hadn't put the car in park before shutting off the engine. I shifted the gear shift lever to the park position and turned the key. The engine roared to life. Throwing the shift lever into gear I propelled the car forward at top speed. Afraid of what I might see I glanced back at the house and sure enough I caught sight of motion and what appeared to be two figures in the library window.

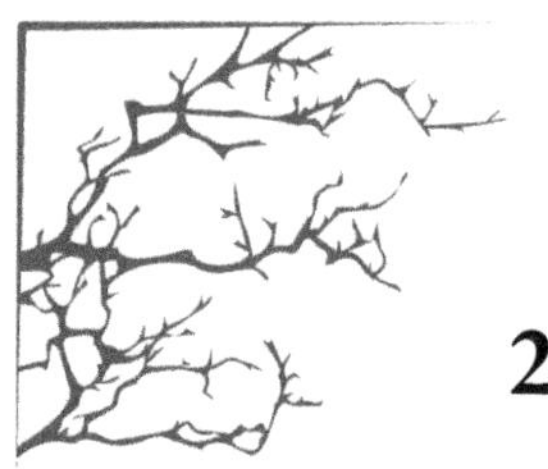

2 A Bewildered Case

Nearing my destination I could see, in the distance, a welcome beacon, glowing yellow against the night sky like the Bat signal, representing a place of protection to those in peril but a symbol of the long arm of the law striking fear in the heart of the most hardened miscreant. I pulled into the parking lot of the provincial police station and after glancing around to make sure no one had followed me in I got out of the car and went to the door only to find it locked, the office deserted for the night.

Walking back to my car I noticed a black full-size SUV, its windows darkly tinted, slowing down as if it was going to turn into the parking lot then changed its mind and sped away.

I didn't know where the nearest pay phone was located and I wasn't going to waste time looking for one or waiting around for them to come back so I got back into my car and headed for the Bonnechance cop shop.

Twenty-five minutes later I stood in front of the Bonnechance cop shop reception's open window, the pong of cigarette smoke from the inner sanctum choking me as I recounted my story to a world-weary receptionist, "... so I didn't waste any time. I got here as fast as I could."

The overweight, middle-aged woman behind the counter, small splotches of ketchup, cheese and coffee adorning her pale blue shirt, raised a bored eyebrow as she handed me an incident report form on a clipboard accompanied by a dime-a-dozen pen on a string and, not even bothering to stifle a yawn, said, "Sit over there." She pointed to a cold, hard wooden bench, dotted with cigarette burns, against the wall. "Write it all down and someone'll look into it. Sign and date it at the bottom of the page." Then she shut the window with a thud and disappeared behind the counter.

I had never been to the police station before. Looking around I noticed dirty hand prints, mud and a plethora of unknown smears on the walls, two metal folding chairs looking worse for wear sat opposite the forlorn wooden bench. Someone had moved the dirt around on the floor with a mop leaving muddy water to dry in swirls on the surface of the terrazzo. Next to the counter was a secure door with a keypad entry system. The base of the door was covered in scuff marks and the wall beside it bore the impression of someone's fist or perhaps their head, the hallmark of a guest resisting the invitation to visit the guest rooms.

I kept one eye on the entrance door as I proceeded to record my afternoon's experience. The prized pen's tatty string tether was too short to allow me to write so I abandoned their fine writing instrument and used my own. Thirty minutes later I had completed my report.

The flickering of the fluorescent lights and my empty stomach were giving me a headache and I was becoming irritable. Returning to the counter I peered through the murky, yellowed glass of the closed window coated with tar, nicotine and fingerprints but could see no one. I noticed a bell next to my hand so I tapped it tentatively and waited. No one appeared so I rapped the bell again, harder this time, and waited. My patience wearing thin I was about to hit the bell again when a bleary-eyed desk sergeant appeared followed by a familiar face, Constable Billy Aiken.

"Hello there, Justin." Billy greeted me heartily. "What brings you here?" he inquired.

"I found a body. Here's my statement." I replied irritably, handing Billy the clipboard with the pen still attached by a piece of string.

"A body! You're joking, right? It's against the law to file a false police report, you know?" Responded a dubious Constable Aiken with a wink as he took the clipboard and read the report. "You're serious?"

"Never more serious," I said while my stomach growled impatiently.

"This is out of my bailiwick. I'll have to call the Prince Edward County detachment of the Provincial Police. You'd better come through." Billy opened the door and ushered me to an interview room to wait for the OPP constables then went to make the call.

Billy returned to the interview room a few minutes later to inform me that, "OPP Detectives are on their way. They'll want to ask you a few questions and then they'll probably take you out to this house where you found the body." Billy gave me a questioning look when my stomach complained rather loudly.

"I haven't eaten since breakfast. My stomach thinks my throat's been cut." I explained.

"Why don't you go across the street and get a burger but be quick about it? They'll be here soon. Ring the bell when you get back and I'll open the door over there for you to come through." Billy indicated the door beside the counter with the keypad entry system.

"Have you forgotten about the sinister-looking SUV that followed me?"

"I'll take a look around. You'll be fine." He assured me as if he was looking under the bed for boogie men for a small child.

Opening the door I peered out into the dimly lit parking lot. Billy stepped outside and not seeing anything suspicious he gave me the all-clear and I left the station in search of sustenance. After wolfing down a cheeseburger, fries and a chocolate milkshake I hurried back to the station. Before I could ring the bell Billy opened the office door and said, "Let's go they're waiting for you."

"Aren't you going with us?" I asked nervously.

"Not my jurisdiction. Two county Mounties will be taking you out to the scene. They have your report and will probably have a few questions for you." Billy assured.

Outside we were met by two detectives in dark grey suits. Billy made the introductions, "Justin Case, this is Homicide Detective Staff Sergeant Oxley Kaye and Homicide Detective Sergeant Beck Nyne." He said purposefully. They'll go with you out to the scene of the alleged incident."

DSS O. Kaye stood about six foot two with a bushy moustache that fluttered when he spoke and the tip of his shabby red tie road on a moderate paunch. A clean-shaven DS Nyne was a very solidly built six foot and sported a paisley tie.

The solemn detectives shook my hand and we got into the patrol car for the long drive back to the lake and the abandoned stately home. "Do you have the instructions you were given concerning your mission?" asked DS Nyne.

I handed him the requisition for the property and he immediately got a map out, sought the location of fire number 1758 and plotted our course.

DSS Kaye turned to look at me and enquired, "What did you say you were doing at this house?"

"I'm under contract to recover the Tin Can Communication Company equipment from locations where the contract has expired or the customer has abandoned the equipment. I never know the reason for a specific termination. I'm just given a list of locations and descriptions of the sets I am to terminate." I explained.

"How do you arrange entry to the premises?" asked Nyne.

"Sometimes there is a note next to an address on the requisition, as was the case with this property. If there is no note I go to the location and if someone is living there I ask them for permission to enter. If the property is unoccupied I try to find the owner or someone authorized to grant me entry. If the property is registered as "For Sale", I make every effort to find an owner, neighbour or real estate agent with authority. If the property is abandoned I go to the municipal office to ask for permission to enter and repossess the Tin Can Communication Company's equipment." I clarified looking somewhat puzzled. "Only..."

"Yes?" said DS Nyne waiting patiently.

"Mrs. Wright, the Registry Office clerk, gave me a key but..." I said removing the key from my pocket and holding it up. "But it wouldn't fit the lock," I said perplexed.

Nyne fell silent as he examined the key. "It looks like a padlock key. Was there a padlock, Mr. Case?" he observed handing the key back to me with a look of suspicion.

"No. There was no padlock on the door."

We were deep in the county when I noticed that DSS Kaye had made a wrong turn. "Uh, sorry Detective Staff Sergeant Kaye but this isn't the way. We should stay on Babylon Road. You've just turned onto Sleepy Hollow Lane."

DSS Kaye looked over at DS Nyne who checked the requisition confirming our course and turned to look at me, "The fire number is 1758, right?"

"That's right but we shouldn't be turning here. When I was here earlier today Sleepy Hollow Lane went straight on." I said pointing.

"It's clear the sign directs us to fire number 1758, does it not, Mr. Case?"

"Y...yes, but..."

"And the requisition clearly states fire number 1758 does it not, Mr. Case?"

"Y...yes, but..."

"So, we must be going the right way. Wouldn't you say, Mr. Case?" He said condescendingly.

"Yes, but there must be something wrong; this is not the way I went."

Within a few minutes, we arrived at our destination. "This is not the house I entered to recover the equipment. I've never been here before."

I spotted a padlock on the door. "Look there's a padlock on the door. There was no padlock on the door of the house I entered. Besides it was a two-story stone mansion, not a brick bungalow."

"Are you certain, Mr. Case? Did you find any equipment belonging to the Tin Can Communications Company?" asked DS Nyne.

"Of course I'm certain and no, I didn't find any TCC equipment. After I discovered the body and heard the sound... Anyway, I didn't stay around to look any further. I just got out of there." I confirmed.

DSS Kaye held out his hand for the key. "Let me have the key."

Kaye used one of his disposable forensics gloves to hold the lock as he inserted the key in the padlock and turned it. Immediately the lock popped open.

"I d...don't understand. I've never been to this house. We're wasting time. The body I saw was in the upstairs front bedroom of the mansion at the end of Babylon Road. I'll show you if you'd only listen." My patience was beginning to wear thin.

"I think we'll take a look around while we're here Mr. Case if it's all the same to you." Said DSS Kaye firmly.

Flashlights at the ready the two county Mounties entered the house. I rummaged in my utility pack for my headlamp and pulling it out strapped it on. Then taking a step as if to follow them inside, I was brought up short, "You wait here. Better yet, Mr. Case, you wait in the car." Ordered the DSS brusquely.

Looking around Kaye noticed the closed circuit camera mounted above the door and realizing it was too late nudged his partner pointing at the video surveillance device and stepped over the threshold onto 1960s harvest gold linoleum flooring. All their senses instantly on high alert they placed their hands on their weapons at the ready, DS Nyne remarked, "Do you smell that?"

"Ya, it smells like fresh paint and ammonia." Replied DSS Kaye.

The small vestibule had a closet ahead to the left with bifold doors and before that to the left was the bare dining room with a doorway off of it leading to the kitchen. Passing the closet there was a door to the left into the kitchen and a hallway to their right that led to three bedrooms and two bathrooms.

The scene that met their eyes in the kitchen was an array of separator funnels, Bunsen burners, reaction vessels, plastic storage containers and glass beakers. The counters and floors were littered with empty containers that had once held acetone, anhydrous ammonia, hydrochloric acid, red phosphorous and sulphuric acid. It had every appearance of a science classroom or a full-scale Methamphetamine laboratory capable of producing multiple pounds of the dangerous drug, a "Super Lab". There was enough equipment to take the process from raw chemicals to a finished product. DS Kaye expressed his astonishment by letting out a low whistle.

"Looks like they cleared out in a hurry." Muttered Kaye.

"They must have been tipped off." Responded Nyne.

Straight ahead of them was the living room devoid of furnishings and the sound of their shoes on the hardwood floor echoed in the emptiness. DSS Kaye motioned for his DS to check out the bedrooms while he explored the basement. Opening the door to the basement his senses were assaulted by the strong odor of skunk. He didn't get more than a few steps down when he realized the entire basement was a marijuana grow operation. Quickly scanning the cellar for any thugs that might be hiding he noticed several shrubs in a separate area with plants he didn't recognize with white flowers hanging down like dangling trumpets that seemed oddly out of place. Satisfied there were no hidden miscreants he shrugged and returned to the main floor.

I grew restless and decided to take a quick look inside despite DSS Kaye's admonition. The acrid smell burned my nose and made me pull my arm up to block out the malodorous stench but to no avail. Entering the kitchen I couldn't believe my eyes and as I looked around the room I spotted a wall-mounted phone on the kitchen wall. Walking into the living room I located a second phone on the floor and finally in the master bedroom I found the third phone. *Well, at least this trip hadn't been a total waste of time.* I thought but just as I was about to disconnect the bedroom phone set there was a harsh voice behind me. "Mr. Case! Do NOT touch anything. This is a crime scene. Did I not give you strict instructions to wait for us in the car?"

"Y...Yes sir. I didn't touch anything Detective Staff Sergeant Kaye. But I'm the one that signed out the key. It's my job to retrieve the phone sets. I won't get paid without them." I whinged pathetically.

"This house and everything in it is evidence of a crime. Where's the body you got us out here to see?" demanded DSS Kaye.

"You haven't been listening to me. This is not the right house. I mean it's the house I was supposed to have gone to, apparently, but it's not the house I ended up at. The sign must have been turned or something. I don't know. All I know for sure is that this is not the house I went to."

"Then how do you explain the fire number?" argued DS Nyne.

"I don't know. I mean I can't. Oh, all I know is this isn't the right house and I did find a body. We need to go back to Babylon Road and follow it to the end."

DS Nyne joined them and DSS Kaye told him to, "Call it in and get the drug squad and forensics here on the double. And get a couple of uniforms here to secure the scene."

"Sir." Acknowledged Nyne, heading to the car to call dispatch to put them in the picture. He instructed them to rally the drug squad, forensics team and to send out a couple of uniforms to secure the scene.

Returning to the house he informed his superior, "I've notified dispatch and the teams are on their way, sir."

"What now?" I asked.

Turning back to me he said, "Now we wait."

"What about the black SUV that followed me?" I asked.

"What black SUV?" grumbled an irritated Kaye.

"I thought a black SUV followed me from the house to the CWPP station. It slowed down and looked like it was going to pull into the parking lot where I was trying to get help." I explained.

"Did you get anything other than just, 'a black SUV'?" enquired Kaye.

"I got a quick look at the plate and it looked like 'I SEE U' but the windows were too dark for me to see any faces. That's all I can tell you. I did put it all in my report." I thought to myself irritably, *Why won't he take me seriously?*

"It sounds like perhaps you were imagining things. Not much to go on in any case, Mr. Case. This better not be a wild-goose chase. There's a law against wasting police time and filing false reports." Warned the DSS.

"What about wasting my time? There should be a law against that." I muttered to myself.

"What was that?" demanded a cantankerous Kaye.

It wasn't long before a "Black and White" lights flashing, pulled to a skidding halt beside the detectives' unmarked car. Two uniformed officers climbed out and hurried up to DSS Kaye seeking their orders.

DS Nyne took the two county Mounties aside to describe the situation and warned them of the hazards. The two men left to take up their posts at the front and rear entrances.

Just as he was finishing with the two officers the forensics van pulled up and the team piled out. DS Nyne explained what had been discovered and that the property had been cleared. The team donned hazardous materials suits and entered the house to set to work.

While DS Nyne had been bringing forensics up to speed two black and whites arrived carrying more boys and girls in blue and two more detectives. After greetings were dispensed with the two senior detectives had a brief exchange during which Kaye handed his counterpart from the drugs squad the key to the bungalow.

Now that the crime scene was in full investigation mode and apparently, the Homicide Detectives were no longer required Kaye returned his attention to me and a little matter of a corpse, "Come with us." He ordered me and we left the bungalow, climbed into the cruiser and headed for Babylon Road.

Arriving back at the junction DS Nyne got out of the car to check the sign which clearly, indicated Babylon Road continued to their right. He twisted the signpost; it turned easily in his grip. After a couple of miles, we came to the end of the road and sure enough, there was the mansion just as I had described it. An enormous tree limb lay across one end of the semi-circle driveway.

DS Nyne got out and inspected the fire number hidden in the vines. Climbing back behind the steering wheel of the cruiser he said with obvious exasperation, "The number on the sign is 666. Why did you enter this house when it was plain to see the number was not the one you were looking for?"

"This is all very confusing. I don't know how or why everything got mixed up. All I know is that the number on the sign was 1758 when I got here. Someone must have switched the signs." I protested.

"Well, show us this body you say you found." Ordered an unconvinced DSS Kaye.

Pulling into the driveway we exited the vehicle and just as I had said there was no padlock. DS Nyne inspected the lock, "This lock has been jimmied, sir. There are tool marks."

"Did you do this, Mr. Case?" demanded DSS Kaye.

"No. It was unlocked when I got here." I asserted indignantly.

I set out to tag along with the detectives as they entered the old house but just as before, "Mr. Case, do I have to handcuff you to the car? You will wait here until we have cleared the premises. Is that clear, Mr. Case?" ordered a very impatient DSS Kaye loudly and irritably.

"Crystal. Be care..." I began but I was too late. DSS Kaye walked straight into the very solid table in the middle of the foyer. "...ful." I finished.

He mumbled something unintelligible, then the two detectives switched on their police issue flashlights upon entering the house. It was black as pitch and quiet as the grave in the old house.

DSS Kaye motioned for the Detective Sergeant to investigate the ground floor while he inspected the upper floor. They both endeavoured to walk softly to avoid alerting anyone lurking unseen in the shadows but their attempts were futile as every footfall echoed throughout the cavernous darkness.

After searching the ground floor and finding nothing dubious he paused in front of the cellar door listening but could not detect any sound of movement. Opening the door a crack he was greeted by the dank odour of damp earth and a whiff of something he couldn't quite put his finger on; wet dog maybe? At that moment he heard DSS Kaye call out for him to join him upstairs. So he closed the door and continued along the hall to the base of the staircase thinking, to himself that he would return and search it thoroughly later.

Hearing his Sergeant's footfalls in the hallway Kaye called out, "In here."

Arriving in the doorway of the bedroom ostensibly containing the corpse Nyne was shocked to find the DSS standing staring at a grisly figure in a rocking chair. "Get him in up here. And call forensics; let them know we've found a body." Kaye ordered his DS.

"Sir," acknowledged his Sergeant.

I was impatiently pacing to and fro outside chomping at the bit to get to the bedroom upstairs to vindicate myself although I was indignantly unsure as to why I should have to. I simmered as I thought about how I was inexplicably made to feel as if I was lying and that I might in some way be responsible.

DS Nyne had just left the bedroom when he heard a loud creak from below the stairs that sounded as if the old house had shrieked in pain. "That sounded like the cellar door. I knew I should have checked the basement. Kaye will have my head for this." He thought, rushing headlong down the main staircase. He glimpsed a flurry of motion in the darkness and, what sounded like the scrabbling of claws on the hardwood floor, as someone or something made a dash for the front door.

"Stop, Police!" yelled DS Nyne.

The fleeing figures burst from the front door immediately colliding head over heels with me bowling me over. We lay in a writhing heap of arms and legs, each fighting to regain our feet. I felt something cold and wet on my cheek then my face was smothered in warm and wet licks. Opening my eyes I found a goofy golden retriever standing over me trying to give me the kiss of life.

The nimble runaway leaped to her feet first. Quickly realizing what had hit me, I flailed about wildly managing to grab hold of her ankle with one hand. The dog, thinking this was a wonderful game, joined in the tug of war by grabbing hold of the fleeing fugitive's pant leg.

"Let go of me you mad, ungrateful, beast!" She shrieked trying to free her leg to make good her escape.

I wasn't sure who she was referring to when she yelled, "Ungrateful, beast".

Just as the frantically wriggling captive was about to slip from my grasp DS Nyne reached our writhing mass of arms and legs. "Alright, break it up." He yelled only to be greeted by a barrage of tiny flailing fists and a cavorting canine, barking as if to cheer them on and who evidently, thought this was great fun.

After a brief mêlée, the detective had his fugitive restrained. "Get your dog under control. What's your name?" he demanded.

"That addle pate is no friend of mine." The more she became agitated the stronger her accent became.

She gave him a look of distinct contempt and with her nose in the air refused to say anything further. "Maybe a night in the cells will loosen your tongue." DS Nyne retorted sternly.

"Heidi Jewels; if you must know. Notcho, **sit,** my unfaithful and ungrateful companion," she spat the words out. Notcho obediently sat and happily wagged her tail, tongue lolling out the side of her mouth and looking from one to the other of her new playmates hoping for more play time and maybe a treat.

"If she's not your dog how do you know her name? What is your business here and why were you hiding?"

"I don't know her name. She's not my dog and she's not your dog so I named her Notcho dog."

I wasn't hiding, was I? Didn't know who you were, did I? Thought you might be yobs up to no good or worse, Jackboots. Sounded like I was outnumbered and..." she looked him up and down "outweighed. Thought if I could leg it I would call the local plod." She griped.

"You didn't hear us announce ourselves, Ms. Jewels and who are these 'Jackboots'?".

"No." She spat.

"Why didn't you stop when I identified myself?" he barked.

Heidi groused, "Anybody can say they're rozzers, can't they? How was I to know?"

"What were you doing in the old house and who the devil are these 'Jackboots and rozzers'?"

"I needed to get out of the storm. I knocked and no one answered so I tried the door, it was unlocked so I went in, didn't I? It's a spooky great pile. It gave me the creeps I can tell you, but beggars can't be choosers, in a storm, as they say. Had a shufty and it looked like no one lived here so I thought I would make the best of it until the storm passed."

"How did you get here? I don't see any vehicle."

"My bicycle is over there in the bushes." She said indicating by nodding her head in the direction of the concealed mode of transport.

Headlights could be seen in the twilight bobbing along the uneven roadway as the black and white made the turn into the driveway where they stood. DSS Kaye appeared in the doorway, hands on his hips, impatiently watching the proceedings. Two officers emerged from the squad car, "Who's this? Did you catch her all by yourself Beck or did you need help?" chuckled the six-foot-six mountain of a man said elbowing his partner almost knocking her over.

"Ya, alright you've had your fun, Kent. She's all yours and watch out, she kicks. Call the Humane Society to pick up the mutt." warned Nyne.

"We'll have none of that missy or we'll put you in leg irons," admonished the big man.

The sergeant held her while his partner put a muzzle on Notcho who sat patiently submitting to the indignity. "Do you have anything in your pockets that will harm me, like knives or needles?" Asked Constable Viola Fuss before she began patting her down and turning out her pockets.

"Oi, get these darbies off me!" She screeched as she strained at the handcuffs. "I wish I did have something to stick you with. Let go of me, you great pillock." Heidi wailed as she thrashed about.

Fuss removed the small backpack Heidi had on her back by undoing the shoulder strap buckles. Donning a pair of gloves she began warily reaching into the wriggling prisoner's pockets with just two fingers removing a crumpled business card for the law firm Dewey, Cheetham & Howe, a penlight, cell phone, a gum wrapper, and twenty dollars which she immediately gave to DS Nyne. She next set to work rummaging in the backpack where she found a change of clothes, a United Kingdom passport, two ten pound notes, a hairbrush, toothbrush, toothpaste and a tattered reprint of 'Picturesque Prince Edward County by Himmler Renell, 1890.

DS Nyne went to his unmarked car and climbing in began tapping on his computer keypad to perform a background check on their prisoner. Within seconds the screen lit up with an insignificant rap sheet of petty theft and misdemeanours. He called out to the uniformed officers, "She's only been in the country a few days and already she has a rap sheet of petty crime and misdemeanours; mostly shoplifting. Probably if we check the serial number on that bicycle we'll find it stolen." He said indicating the bike in the bushes.

"I had to eat, didn't I" shouted their feisty prisoner.

DSS Kaye had made his way down to the group, ruffled Notcho's head fondly and looking at me said, "One more question, Mr. Case. You said the door to the bedroom was locked from the inside?"

"That's right."

"Would you mind telling me how you got into a locked room?"

"The key was still in the lock on the inside so I slipped my map under the door and pushed it out with my screwdriver. I slid my map out from under the door and used the key to unlock the door."

"You can ride back to town with Sergeant Good. We won't be needing you anymore tonight." And turning to the Sergeant he said, "Take the prisoner to the station and lock her up for the night."

"Yes Sir" acknowledged Good. "What do you want me to do with the dog, sir?"

"I'll take Notcho, if I may?" I offered.

DSS Kaye thought for a moment then acquiesced, "Yes, yes, alright. Just get her out of here before I change my mind. Remove that muzzle. She can ride in the back with Miss Jewels." He didn't want to let on he had a soft spot for dogs, especially labs.

"Yes sir," replied the Sergeant nodding.

"Constable Fuss."

"Sir," she responded curtly.

"The body is in the upstairs bedroom at the front of the house on the right. I want you outside the bedroom door to secure the crime scene."

"Body?!" exclaimed Heidi.

"Yes Sir," Fuss replied turning on her heel and heading for the front door.

"Yes, Miss Jewels, a body. Do you know anything about what happened here?" questioned DSS Kaye.

"I don't know anything about a body. It's nowt to do with me." Heidi replied.

"Hmm, we'll see about that. On your way Sergeant."

I climbed into the squad car next to Sergeant Kent B. Good and we headed back to town.

DSS Kaye stood with one hand rubbing his neck in consternation watching the squad car's tail lights bob and weave its way down the rutted lane. He said to DS Nyne, "What did you think of Case?"

"It seems he was telling the truth. I think he was unwittingly directed to the wrong address to steer him away from the drugs lab, Sir."

"Ya, that's what I thought, what do you make of the girl?"

"I think she's hiding something and maybe a night in the cells will convince her to share whatever it is with us."

"Hmmm, What are we missing, Nyne? Something's nagging at me but what?"

Nyne had seen his boss like this before and knew he'd be as grumpy as an old bear with an itch he can't quite reach until he found a way to scratch it.

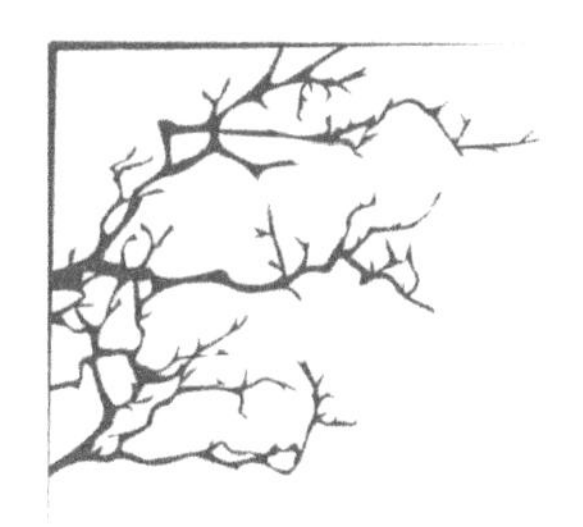

3 gone fishing

The rest of the week passed uneventfully and Tippy, my parents' black lab, had enjoyed sharing her home with her new golden-haired companion. I live with my parents in a modest home in the Village of Ameliasburgh[1] overlooking a peaceful valley and mill pond. Not wanting to invade Tippy's space Notcho and I stayed in my father's large workshop out back of the main house. It was warm and cozy and smelled of freshly sawn lumber.

I called DS Nyne and learned that Heidi Jewels had been released but couldn't or wouldn't tell me any more than that.

The weekend rolled around as they often do. It was Friday night and I was meeting my friends: Lawson, Hugo, Nick, Nack, and Moose at Lawson's to go smelt fishing off the shore of North Beach. Pulling into Lawson's driveway I shut off the engine and got out. "You stay here, Notcho. I won't be long." Notcho cocked her head trying to understand what I was saying to her then lay down to patiently wait for my return.

Lawson had scrounged a seine net from somewhere. It was checked over for tears and Lawson explained how it was to be used.

"I spoke to Billy Aiken the other day and you'll never guess what happened to me," I said expectantly.

Everyone continued their good-natured kibitzing as they prepared for the night of fishing as if they hadn't heard me. Perhaps they hadn't heard me but to repeat myself would appear to be desperate for them to listen. At first, I felt hurt and inadequate then I was annoyed thinking to myself, "Fine they aren't interested. Perhaps it's not worth telling, anyway. You'd think I'd be used to this by now.

I've always felt as if I was on the periphery of my friends, an observer."

Nack seemed to notice that something was bothering me and taking pity on me asked, "What happened to you the other day? Did Billy have to give you a ticket?"

"It was no big deal and no he didn't give me a ticket. It's okay Nack, thanks for asking. We should get going. We don't want to miss the first run." I said with mixed emotions. I was embarrassed that Nack felt he had to take pity on me and I was angry because I wondered how I thought they were my friends but would friends treat you with such indifference? I did want to tell my story but not to friends that listened either out of sympathy or grudgingly. I knew it was my fault for not being as dynamic as Hugo, Lawson and Nick. They hadn't even realized how I felt. Oh well, this too shall pass. They all had their minds on more important things, like catching smelts.

I soon forgot about the snub by my friends, as I always did, and got caught up in the new adventure. Nick threw the net and the gear into the back of his station wagon and then got in behind the wheel while Nack, Hugo and our painfully thin, friend we affectionately referred to as Moose, piled into their seats for the ride. I climbed in behind the wheel of my Mustang. Lawson opened the passenger door and was greeted by a cold wet nose. Notcho beat a tattoo on the back of my seat with her tail as she wriggled and wiggled in her excitement going from one to the other sniffing and kissing.

"When did you get a dog?" asked Lawson wiping slobber from his face.

"This is Notcho. She's not mine. She's just visiting. Have you been talking to Billy lately?" I queried.

"No. Why? What's that got to do with you getting a dog?" replied Lawson.

"Oh, I just wondered if he had told you about the excitement in the county this week," I said hoping to stir further curiosity.

"You mean the dead body found in an old house and the drug lab the police uncovered? I saw something in the Bonnechance Dispatch. Why? That's not Billy's jurisdiction. And what's that got to do with your new dog?" It was obvious I had piqued Lawson's curiosity.

"Well, I discovered the body when I went to this big, dark old abandoned house to recover three phone sets. It seems that the street sign and fire numbers had been switched and the house I should have gone to was the drug lab and grow op."

Lawson was a quick thinker and asked, "How did they know to change the street sign and fire numbers?" taking me by surprise.

"Wow. I hadn't thought of that. That's a very good question." I responded at a complete loss.

"Who was the dead body? How did they die?" wondered an incredulous Lawson out loud.

"The police are still investigating but whoever it was looked like they had been dead for quite a while," I replied while digging in my pocket. "A girl, Heidi Jewels, had been hiding in the cellar of the old house and made a run for it with Notcho hot on her heels. They ran into me and I caught her by the leg. I guess Notcho thought it was a game because she grabbed hold of the girl's pant leg and started tugging. The police handcuffed the girl and took her away. They were going to call the Humane Society for Notcho and I asked if I could take her home and they let me." I explained, my words tumbling out but somehow sounding inane.

"Sometime during the scuffle she must have slipped these into my pocket," I said holding up a gold Louis XV Louis D'Or.

"Is that real gold?" asked a wide-eyed Lawson.

"I...I think so. I looked it up and if it's real it's worth about one thousand, two hundred U.S. dollars. I also found a folded piece of paper"

"Where did she get the coin? What's on the paper?" he asked, his curiosity aroused and then suddenly alarmed, "You better turn it all over to the police. That could be withholding evidence." Warned Lawson.

"Ya, I suppose I should. I'll take it down tomorrow but how else would we be able to find the treasure?"

"Treasure, what treasure?" exclaimed Lawson.

"Ya, I didn't know about it either. There's believed to be a treasure buried at the Outlet?" Lawson shot me a look of disbelief. "Yup, in 1758 the British were chasing a French gunboat and the French knew they were about to be caught so they burned their boat and buried a barrel of gold," I told him.

Lawson fell silent for a moment mulling over what he had just heard but couldn't resist, "What's on the paper?"

"An old map of what looks like the Outlet with an "X" marked on it very close to the western end of the river and a poem.

The gold, how it shone
right where you left it, gone.
Waiting for the light
hidden in plain sight.
No longer gold

Many stories are told.

"What's that supposed to mean?" asked Lawson.

"I have no idea," I replied as we pulled to a stop at the edge of an expanse of flat rock on the shore of the lake. Everybody got to work putting on hip waders and getting flashlights and garbage bags ready. The light from our flashlights would attract the smelts into our net. We'd scoop up the silvery catch and dump them into the garbage bags to take home for cleaning.

The night was cold and clear with a watery, bluish-white moon shining like a beacon, its light shimmering on the surface of a gently undulating lake. Millions of twinkling stars filled a black velvet sky. I nudged Nick, who stood gazing up at the sky, and said with a wink, "What if those aren't stars but pin holes in a lid to let air in?"

His initial reaction was one of vagueness then he chuckled and we set to work unrolling and dipping the net. It wasn't long before our net had been filled and emptied several times and it was time to go home to clean the tiny spring treat.

Notcho busied herself sniffing each of the guys and exploring her surroundings. She seemed puzzled by this new game we played and tried to rescue the tiny creatures that had escaped the net flipping and flopping on the flat rock by gently picking them up in her mouth and putting them back in the water.

Hugo, Nack, Nick and Moose each took their share of the spoils and left for home while Lawson and I headed back to Lawson's father's workshop to clean the rest of the slippery, silver bounty. "I've never had smelts before. How do you clean them and cook them?" I asked.

"Take off their heads and clean out the guts then just fry 'em up with butter and salt." Suggested Lawson.

"Any idea how he died?" he asked deep in thought going over everything that I had told him earlier.

"He was murdered."

How do you know?"

"His hands and feet were bound to the chair and he was covered by a sheet that the wind blew off.

And before you ask, I have no idea how he was murdered. All I know is the room was locked from the inside and there was no other way out of the room." I paused to ponder whether or not to mention the uncanny feathered harbinger. "There was one other weird thing."

"What could be weirder than finding a body tied to a chair in a locked room?" he asked incredulously.

"A bird."

"What's weird about a bird?"

"It spoke. A big black crow or raven appeared on the windowsill and spoke. Then it slipped between the bars and disappeared into the night."

"You sure it didn't just sound like talking? What did it say?" he asked doubtfully.

"It said, "murdrum". I said apprehensively.

"That doesn't even sound like a word. You sure you weren't imagining it?"

"I have no idea what it means if it means anything at all." I mused.

With that, we fell silent, lost in thought, for the rest of the journey.

Upon our arrival at Lawson's place, I spotted a bicycle leaning against the wall of the workshop. It was identical to the one that the girl from the old house had hidden in the bushes. "I think we may have company Lawson," I said pointing to the bike. "That's Heidi Jewels' bike. What's she doing here?"

"Probably wants the coin and map back."

"I can't let her have them. They're evidence. I've got to take them to the police. What can I do?" I protested.

Lawson simply shrugged. "It's your call."

I brought my car to a stop outside the door of the workshop just as Heidi came out of the door looking tired and cold. "What are you doing here? I called DS Nyne and he said you had been released but couldn't tell me how I could get in touch with you." I queried suspiciously.

"I was in jail but they couldn't pin anything on me so they had to let me go. I followed you here earlier this evening. After you all left I hung around until you came back. Who's your friend?" asked Heidi, eyeing Lawson's muscular physique and smiling eyes set in his chiselled face looking for any sign of an opportunity to make an ally.

Before us, stood a disarmingly petite creature with a turned-up button nose and silky chestnut hair in a pixie-style hairdo; her eyes shone like the warm golden, coppery glow from amber lanterns as they reflected the light from the workshop.

"Aren't you going to introduce us?" asked Lawson who proceeded to introduce himself, "I'm Lawson, Lawson D. Woods. You must be Heidi Jewels. I've heard a lot about you."

To Lawson, she said, "Has he been spreading lies about me?" her lower lip protruding in an appealing pout. She didn't wait for a response. "You look like a fair-minded person. What's he been saying about me? He doesn't even know me." And to me, she said with a smouldering look, "Oi, where's my clobber? 'And it over, it's mine."

"It's not yours. You probably stole it. Besides, it's evidence. We need to turn it over to the police." I argued. "Why did you come running out of the cellar like that anyway?"

"I heard the bizzies talking about searching the cellar next so I knew I had to scarper. I didn't know you'd be in my way, did I?

Now, give me my things and I'll be on my way."

"How did you find that place? Did the sign say Babylon Road or Sleepy Hollow Lane? What was the fire number? What were you looking for?" I questioned.

"Whoa, slow down there. You sound just like the rozzers. What are you, some kind of old Bill wanna-be? Give me my coin and paper and I'll tell you everything I know." She bargained.

"No way. You'll take it and run."

She glowered at me, "Ok, ok.

First, I wasn't looking for that place. I was just looking for a place to kip for a while and I found that creepy old place. Beggars can't be choosers I said to myself.

The sign said, Babylon Road and I didn't notice the fire number. Now, give me my stuff and I'll be off." She said, with an expression of petulant annoyance.

"What's the poem mean?"

"What poem? How should I know? I haven't even had a chance to look at the paper myself."

"What if we copy the page and then turn it in?" Lawson interjected.

"What about my coin?" whinged Heidi. "You said if I answered your questions you'd hand over my clobber."

Ignoring Heidi's protests I said, "That's a good idea, Lawson."

"Oi, don't I get a say?"

"No!" we both said in unison.

We made plans to photocopy the document first thing in the morning subsequently turning everything over to the proper authorities.

"We need to get these fish cleaned before they go off." Lawson reminded me.

We set to work cleaning our catch while Heidi, having made up her mind not to let whoever held the coin and treasure map out of her sight, settled down for a long night.

The first warming rays of dawn were just beginning to creep over the window sill as Lawson and I finished cleaning the last of the bite-size fish. Stretching and yawning I reflected out loud, "I wonder where our tiny trespasser has gotten to?

You take the letter and coin and tuck it away for safekeeping while we both get a couple of hours' sleep."

Lawson agreed this was a good plan, "Meet me back here at 10:00 am and we'll go to the library to copy the map then to the police station."

Upon reaching my car I snuck a quick look inside and discovered Heidi curled up in the passenger seat peacefully sleeping with a slight smile on her lips as if she was enjoying a private joke and a dribble of drool on her chin. She gave the impression of being so deceptively gentle and vulnerable, contrary to reality. I quietly opened the driver's door to my Mustang, trying not to wake her. I had hoped to avoid her relentless wheedling but Notcho spotted her friend and before I could stop her she scrambled into the seat beside her, wiggling and wagging her tail a mile a minute. Notcho lavished Heidi's face with kisses causing her to sit bolt upright straight away, wide awake and ready to fend off an attack but not ready for Notcho.

I was immediately greeted with, "Where's my stuff?"

"Well, good morning to you too," I said sarcastically. "It's in a safe place until the library opens then we'll photocopy the map as we agreed and then turn everything over to the police. You might want to wipe your chin." I said.

"I didn't agree to anything." She snapped touchily wiping at her chin.

"Where would you like me to drop you off?"

"I'm going with you. I have no place else to go." She said folding her arms across her chest petulantly.

Hesitating, "I'll have to check with my parents." I said grudgingly.

"You still live with your parents?"
"It's convenient," I said embarrassed.

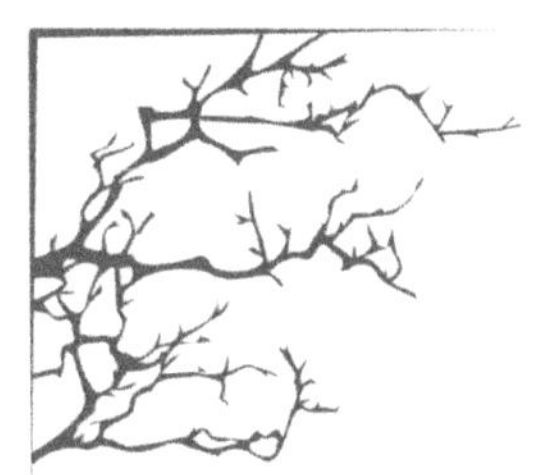

4 love, lies & legacy

You have to be an optimist to open your eyes when you wake up in the morning. But this morning was different. There were culinary sounds of bacon sizzling and spitting in the frying pan and the drip, drip, burble, and hiss of the coffee percolator as it brewed the deep, dark, rich sanity in a cup. "I want to live my life in such a way that when I get out of bed in the morning, the devil says, 'aw crap, he's up! But who could be surly with the tantalizingly mouth-watering aromas of bacon frying, tea biscuits baking and the nutty aroma of coffee brewing filling my apartment." I reflected as I clambered from my bed.

Wrapping my housecoat around me I made my way to the kitchen where I encountered a scene of domestic bliss. Heidi and my mother appeared to have bonded. A bowl coated in remnants of biscuit batter and another coated with eggs, a measuring cup, spoons of all sizes and a mixing whisk littered the counter. Flour and various and sundry other ingredients too numerous to mention adorned every flat surface and dripped from the edges.

Notcho lay on the floor next to Tippy their dishes looking like they were in contemplation, "We're being starved. We haven't eaten a thing for an hour."

I stood in the doorway with a goofy look of amazement on my face. "Well, good morning. Wow! Everything looks or, well uh um, smells amazing." I greeted, for the second time that day, hoping for a more jovial response from Heidi this time.

She overlooked my incredulity and just smiled self-consciously at my praise, "Well, I was hungry, wasn't I? Your guests must die of starvation waiting for you to get a meal.

Help yourself. I'm not going to serve you. I'm going to take a shower." Popping a morsel of bacon into her mouth and one into Notcho's and Tippy's she turned on her heel and left the room.

I called out, "The towels are..."

"I know where they are. I've got everything I need. Your Mum has been very helpful." She replied brusquely.

"Thanks, Mum." My mother simply smiled.

Half an hour later Heidi returned to the kitchen looking refreshed. I was just finishing cleaning up. "You are full of surprises," I said.

Looking down at her feet she responded, "I figured I owed you for letting me stay here and your mother is so kind.

What were *you* doing in the old house, anyway?"

"I'm a Termination Agent for the Tin Can Communications Company. I recover equipment belonging to them. I had a requisition to repossess equipment from the house at 1758 Sleepy Hollow Lane. Someone had switched the signs and fire numbers and I ended up at the old house you were in.

You didn't know anything about the corpse upstairs?"

"No. I had a shifty about the old place but that door was locked. Then you showed up so I hid in the cellar."

"Did you happen to see a big black bird?"

"Nope; why?"

"There was one in the bedroom and it could talk."

"Go on with ya. You're pullin my leg. What did it say..." she said with a smirk, "and how did you get into that room anyway?"

"It said just one very bizarre word, "murdrum. I have no idea if it even is a word." I replied ignoring her query about how I gained entry to the locked chamber of horror.

"Murdrum, that's an old English law that means to kill someone in a secret manner differing from a simple homicide."

"Wow! And you know this how?"

"I was reading the History of Law in England at Oxford among other subjects before I came over here." She said knocking me for six.

"You are full of surprises," I exclaimed. "We better get going Lawson will be wondering where we are."

The crisp morning air was filled with the sights, sounds and smells of spring. Lawson watched a robin with its rusty orange breast tug on an earthworm in the wet grass of his front lawn and heard the cold, harsh squawk of a blue jay somewhere nearby. As he sat on the porch of his parents' house he pondered the puzzles I had presented, “Why did someone change the road sign and fire number and how did they know that someone was coming?

How was a murder committed in a locked room?

Were the murderer and the person or persons that changed the signs the same?”

A cerulean blue mustang, with sunlight glinting off of the myriad metallic flecks like tiny sparks in the evening sky, turned into his driveway. He stood and stepped up to the driver’s window as I pulled to a stop. “What time do you call this?”

“Jump in, we’re burning daylight,” I replied.

Heidi opened her door, got out and folded her seat forward to allow Lawson to get into the back seat. “I thought you’d never get here,” Lawson said to me. Climbing into the back seat he greeted Heidi, “Good morning Heidi.”

“Where’s my letter and coin?” demanded an impatient Heidi.

“I can see nothing’s changed.” He said holding up the items for Heidi to see then quickly snatching them away as she tried to grab them.

She “Harrumphed.” In exasperation and slumped in her seat sulkily. Then as if in desperation she pleaded, “If I tell you the truth can I trust you both to keep it just between us?”

I looked at Lawson in the rearview mirror.

Lawson looked at me and I nodded my agreement, “We can’t make any promises but if we don’t have to tell the police you can count on us.”

“It looks like I don’t have any choice, do I? I guess I have to trust someone but you must promise me to keep what I am about to tell you to yourselves.”

I was about to commit to silence when Lawson spoke up, “We can’t make any promises until we hear what you have to say.”

“Well, my old Mum, Ruby Precious Jewels, passed away recently but before she did she gave me a box and told me I would find my heritage and my birthright. Inside I found a sort of love story, this paper and the gold coin. She passed before I could ask her what it all meant and what I was to do with it.”

“What made you decide to come to Canada?” asked Lawson.

"This letter came for my Mum while I was there.” She handed Lawson the missive.

The letter was on fine quality, expensive stationery with the letterhead of Dewey, Cheetham & Howe, Barristers & Solicitors; and signed by Hugh Louis

Dewey, B.A., M.B.A., L.L.B., Estate Specialist. The substance of the letter, addressed to Mrs. Jewels, read as follows:

"To the heir, legatees and devises of the aforementioned estate:

This letter is to inform you that Longue John Silver III, of 666 Babylon Road, Prince Edward County in the Province of Ontario, died on, May 10, 1969. You have been named in the petition as a possible sole heir with a legal interest in the decedent's estate.

Mr. Hugh Louis Dewey, Esq. of 1 Donald Avenue, County of Prince Edward, Ontario, has been named as the administrator of the estate.

Documents, information and petitions are on file in the above-listed court under the above-listed case number.

Any heir or legatee is entitled to administrative information concerning the decedent's estate."

"When I read this letter and this tale of amour and treasure I knew I must travel to Canada as soon as possible to claim my birthright." She said after rummaging in her pack and retrieving a small dog-eared and ragged manuscript.

She began to read, "In the summer of 1758 Colonel Oliver D. Map sailed from the mouth of the Aswego River to attack Fort Fromtheback; then held by Poupon De Grasse for France. As the British ships neared the Upper Gap a French gun-boat was seen beating up against the wind for the Gap.

Two of Map's ships were sent forward to intercept the gunboat. The French vessel being unable to reach Fort Faulty changed her course to the west, with Map's vessels in hot pursuit.

The race was an exciting one for about thirty miles, but the English vessels were gradually closing up the distance between them, and as the gunboat was no match for the enemy, her captain decided to save his crew and a barrel of gold he had on board. Accordingly, he rounded Fish Point, sailed up the Outlet, buried the gold in a marked spot, burned his ship to the water's edge and returned overland only to find Fort Faulty taken and destroyed.

Such is the legend that has maintained itself most sturdily in the locality for a century. Perhaps it would have passed into oblivion before this if it had not been for an incident that happened about half a century ago.

One bright summer day some fishermen winding up their nets at Fish Point observed a strange vessel cautiously feeling her way along that dangerous shore.

Creeping along, with the sounding line going, she anchored in the mouth of the Outlet and dropped her sails. It was an unusual thing for a vessel to come in there, and as there was considerable filibustering along the frontier at the time, the fishermen drew near to ascertain what particulars they could about the suspicious stranger. Her crew consisted of only six or seven men, two of whom soon came ashore. One was an ordinary sailor, the other, who interests us more, was about thirty years old, a handsome dark-complexioned gentleman, whose military bearing, neat clothes and polished shoes, somewhat overawed the rough fishermen. He left much of his conversation to his companion, and when he did speak it was with a decided French accent. After enquiring about Captain Silver and learning where they would find him, they returned to their ship, and the fishermen to their homes, vainly surmising who the strangers might be.

That evening M. De Pompadour called on Captain Silver. The two gentlemen were soon together in the best parlour, looking over old maps, sketches and documents yellowed with age. Needless to say, the stranger's mission was about the barrel of gold. He was a descendant of the commander of the gunboat who had hidden the treasure there some eighty years before, and the documents he produced disclosed the exact spot where the treasure lay. Captain Silver promised him all the assistance he could afford and offered him the hospitality of his house while he remained in the neighbourhood, which might be for some time. M. De Pompadour declined with many thanks, as he had, he said, excellent accommodation on his boat and preferred to remain with his men.

While these two are in the parlour another couple is in the dining room who claims our attention for a moment. One is Claude Hopper, a tall, fine-looking man, son of a neighbouring farmer; the other is the Captain's daughter, Precious Silver, as sweet a specimen of young womanhood as any man could aspire to. After an hour's conversation in the parlour M. De Pompadour re-entered the dining room, was introduced to the lovers, made a stately bow and departed, promising to see the Captain on the morrow.

In a few days, the Frenchman and his men had located the spot where the gold was hidden, but he found on examination he had not brought with him all the necessary machinery, and while the boat was absent he was the guest of Captain Silver. It was not Precious' fault that she fell in love with the affable and polished stranger. His knowledge was so wide, his accomplishments so varied, and his presence so charming that he came like a revelation to her somewhat contracted world. But she would not admit M. De Pompadour as a lover as long as she was betrothed to Claude.

But Claude was too busy just now to notice the intimacy growing up between Precious and her guest. If Claude had one fault more prominent than another it was his passion for gain, the mean ambition of getting rich for the mere sake of being rich; and the thought of that immense treasure at the bottom of the river, so near him all these years, and now this stranger was to carry it away, worried him.

One night about dark as M. De Pompadour was returning to his boat he overtook Claude on the Sand Banks, and the two walked on together. The stranger had just left Precious. Claude had just left the buried treasure, and each was engrossed with his own, thoughts. Claude was wondering if he could propose some kind of partnership in the barrel of gold and ventured timidly towards the subject. At the same moment, M. De Pompadour was thinking how he could best sound Claude's feelings towards Precious, so he shifted the conversation by telling Claude he had a much greater treasure in his sweetheart than lay buried in the river. It would be too long a story to follow up the conversation, but before they parted that night they had entered into a solemn compact by which M. De Pompadour was to release to Claude all his right to the gold, and Claude was to release Precious from her engagement. The contract was carried out and in about ten days the strange vessel that had attracted so much attention weighed anchor, spread her sails and departed with Monsieur and Madame De Pompadour.

Claude spent much time and money trying to recover the buried treasure, but all his efforts were unsuccessful, and his friends and neighbours did not regret the result when they learned he traded off his sweetheart for a barrel of gold.[2]

That's it then."

Lawson and I looked at each other and I said, "If it wasn't found at the crime scene I don't think we have to give it to the police. What do you think Lawson?"

"Ya, that sounds about right."

"What do we do now, Lawson?"

"I need a coffee," Lawson replied, handing the poem and coin back to Heidi, who accepted them hesitantly.

"Don't you want to make copies? Aren't you going to help me?" she asked with genuine alarm in her voice.

I started the car, gravel crunched beneath the tires as we rolled out of the driveway. "Where are we going now?" queried Heidi.

"Lawson and I are going for a coffee. I can drop you off wherever you want."

"I want you to drop me and my bicycle off at 666 Babylon Road." She said with a mixture of irritation and disappointment.

"You can get out right here if you'd like, pick up your bike and peddle out to the house. We need to think. I don't want to get into any more trouble than I am already."

She sat silent for a long moment before speaking then looking appealingly from one to the other of us pleading, "I truly need your help, please. I'm all alone in a foreign country with no money. You can't just turn your backs and drive away, please."

"Okay. Okay. I guess it wouldn't hurt to take another look around that spooky old mansion. Are you up for it Lawson or do you want me to drop you off here and I'll take her out to the house?" I said resignedly.

"Ya, I'll go along for the ride but coffee first." Lawson agreed, settling into his seat for a long ride while Notcho stuck her head out the window sniffing the air with her tongue lolling and ears flapping in the wind.

Before leaving Bonnechance we stopped for two coffees and a cuppa. We drove on in silence, each of us savouring our steaming hot beverage of choice and each deep in thought, until finally, Lawson broke the tension, "That's quite a tale. Is that old house Captain Silver's home?" he asked. "I guess if your mother was the sole heir it belongs to you if you're not too late." he pondered to himself out loud.

"The lawyer will know. We'll have to wait until Monday to check." I suggested. "We can check the title of the property with Mrs. Eileen Wright at the Prince Edward County Land Registry Office Monday. There's something odd about that woman but I can't quite put my finger on it." I thought out loud.

"I have an appointment with the Solicitor, Mr. Dewey, Monday morning. It's been such a long time, I wonder if anyone else has come forward for the estate?" She said.

"Well, that's a big step in the right direction," I said.

Notcho's ears flapped in the wind that buffeted the car as we sped along the Prince Edward County back roads. Lawson watched the fence posts flash by as we drove deeper into the county. The closer we got to our destination the narrower the road became until the pavement petered out and the road became a grassy track just as we came in sight of the rocky shore with the wind-whipped lake beyond. The gloomy old stone edifice stood forlorn against a cold, gray and foreboding sky.

The ragged remnants of police crime scene tape flapped and fluttered in the wind like incongruous festive black and yellow bunting. I pulled the mustang to a stop on the drive in front of the main door. We all got out of the car and I handed Lawson a flashlight, "Here. You're going to need this."

We mounted the steps to the front door but just as we were about to enter the door burst open. Before we had time to react we were set upon by three attackers. Lawson was the quickest to recover, scrambling to his feet like a shot. His fists of granite flew like jack hammers and his tall, burly assailant hit the ground like a ton of bricks. He turned his attention to me. I had managed to get to my feet and was grappling with a rotund opponent who flailed frantically as I held him with one arm around his throat in a vice-like hold. Notcho had his ankle in a bone-crushing grip growling menacingly through clenched teeth.

"Haalp! Let me go. You're choking me! I can't breathe!" squealed the hapless hooligan.

Heidi had been knocked for six and sent sprawling into a patch of tall dead brambles in what had long since ceased to be a flourishing garden beside the front porch. She sprang to her feet as if propelled by a powerful unseen coiled spring. The remaining mugger without a dance partner went into paroxysms of laughter as he watched Heidi fall into the flower bed. But he stood mouth agape as she rose into the air in a graceful pirouette. His mirth quickly evaporated when the side of her right foot caught him just behind his right ear. The big man collapsed in a heap onto the concrete porch and was silent.

Frozen in amazement we watched as Heidi brushed herself off and picked leaves and thorns from her clothes and hair, spitting and spluttering.

"Who are you and what do you want?" demanded Lawson of the only attacker still conscious.

"Make them let go. Call your guard dog off! The vicious cur is going to rip my leg off," gurgled the terrified thug.

"First you tell us who you are and what you're doing here?" repeated Lawson.

"Th... that's my brother Remy and I... I'm Romulus Roman. Me and my brother, Remos, and our friend, Isadore Bell" he said pointing to the still comatose vandal "are looking for **our** gold. Are you okay Remy? What have you done to Izzie?" He whined.

"**Your** gold? Your fervent, misguided sense of entitlement is stunning," shouted Heidi.

"Th...That's right, **our** gold. We're descendants of Poupon De Grasse, Commander of Fort Fromtheback, on our mother's side. The gold was meant for him before the English spoiled it." He groused. "What business is it of yours, anyway? I think you broke my nose." Whimpered a groggy, Remos Roman, rubbing his jaw and getting unsteadily to his feet. Lawson took a step in Remy's direction and the thug raised his hands in capitulation.

"You are trespassing on private property, my property, and I want you off." shrieked Heidi.

"Have a little patience, Heidi" cautioned Lawson.

"Patience is what you have when there are too many witnesses" Rejoined Heidi. "Now, leave or I'll call the coppers and have you charged with trespassing."

"Who are you to be ordering us off this property" Remy whinged resentfully.

"This house and land have been in my family for more than five generations if you must know. Now get off my land before I set the local plod on you." She replied indignantly.

Lawson nodded to me and I released the rotund Romulus Roman and I pulled Notcho away. The portly oaf rubbed his throat, gasping and coughing. He limped away to join the other two trudging sulkily around the house to their black SUV with tinted windows. "You haven't seen the last of us. We won't give up what's ours that easily." Remy yelled from the safety of the open window spinning the familiar SUV's tires, spraying gravel as they rounded the house and shot out of the drive narrowly missing my cherished Mustang.

I recognized the SUV as the same one that followed me to the police station the other night.

"I'm glad you're going to see that lawyer, Hugh Dewey, first thing tomorrow to sort out the will," I said leading the way back to the front of the house. "You want to take a look around, Lawson, before we go back to town?"

"Might as well." My friend replied climbing the steps.

"You'll need a flashlight," I said as I went to the car to retrieve three powerful torches.

Heidi was already through the door. "You need a good lock on this door. It's pitch black in here. We need to get some tools and get the boards off of the windows to let some light in." He said scanning the entryway and rooms on either side with his flashlight.

"Why do you think the treasure is here? There's nothing in the story to say it was ever found." Asked Lawson.

"Remember the poem?

The gold, how it shone
right where you left it, gone.
Waiting for the light
hidden in plain sight.
No longer gold
Many stories are told.

The second line "right where you left it. Gone" I think means it's no longer where it was buried. And, "hidden in plain sight" could mean it can be seen if we look in the right place. This seemed like the logical place to start."

"You need to get your legal ducks in a row before you find the treasure." Advised Lawson.

"Let's go get something to eat. My stomach thinks my throat's been cut. After lunch, we can pick up a couple of new locks to secure the doors, front and back." I suggested. We had missed lunch and my stomach was beginning to growl.

After our sub sandwiches, we returned to the old house and Lawson installed the new bronze mortise entry locks both front and back securing the property the best we could for the time being but now it was time to head home. The wind coming off the lake felt soft, warm and full of moisture. The sky was beginning to darken as we got into the car and headed back to Bonnechance. Lawson broke the pensive silence hanging like a cloud over the trio, "I'm golfing with Nack, Nick and Hugo tomorrow. I'll give you a call sometime tomorrow to see how things go."

"Are you all on holiday?" I asked.

I cringed as he replied, "Me and Nack are but Hugo doesn't go in to work until 4:00 and Nick's taking the day off." Turning to Heidi he asked, "What will you do if you find out the house is yours?"

Heidi looked wistful as she considered the question. "What do you mean, '*if* the house is mine'? I know it is. I also know I cannot afford to keep it unless I find the treasure. It's my heritage and if I am the only one left it's up to me to preserve it."

5 looking for gold in all the wrong places

The next morning found Heidi, Notcho and me on the road to a meeting with H. L. Dewey, Esquire, senior partner in the firm of Dewey, Cheetham and Howe, LLB. The brilliant sunlight made me squint. The storm clouds had lifted leaving behind a bright blue sky and the air fresh and clear. I hoped that was a metaphor for the rest of our undertaking.

Lawson, Nack, Nick and Hugo arrived early at the Birch Valley Golf & Country Club. After checking in they went to the restaurant for coffee. Once they were seated Nack, Nick and Hugo listened intently as Lawson regaled them with his exploits from the day before. He concluded with, "...I never saw anything like it. She was like a ninja. That guy never knew what hit him."

His listeners sat open-mouthed. "Wow! So, what now?" asked Nack.

"Justin and Heidi are going to see the lawyer that sent her mother the letter to find out if she has a claim to the property."

"I know that place," said Hugo.

"She's going to need some help to open it up. Who's up for taking a ride out there after our round?" Lawson asked.

"I am, Lawson," offered Nick.

"Ya, me too," Nack agreed.

"Sure. I gotta meet this ninja," said Hugo, chuckling.

Meanwhile, I managed to find the law offices of Dewey, Cheetham and Howe, LLB, located at 1 Donald Avenue. I parked the Mustang next to a black Jaguar Vanden Plas with the licence plate, DCH LLB and we got out and went into the law office. We entered a two-storey, red brick, Greek Revival house circa 1835. The highly polished chestnut floors creaked, echoing off of the high ceilings. Looking around I admired the intricate crown mouldings and vintage panelling.

The syrupy sweet voice of the secretary, whose desk nameplate announced her name was, Miss Levinia Onholde, Receptionist, greeted us, "May I help you?"

"I'm here to see Mr. Dewey," responded Heidi.

"Your name please and just what is your business with Mr. Dewey?"

"My name is Heidi Jewels and I'm here because my Mum, Ruby Precious Jewels, received a letter from your guv'nor about the estate of Mr. Longue John Silver III." The secretary's eyebrow shot up and her mouth fell open as if taken by surprise.

She lifted the receiver on her phone, touched a button and in a barely audible voice announced Heidi's presence to someone on the other end of the line, presumably Mr. Dewey. "You can go right up. His office is the second door on the left at the top of the stairs."

We climbed the stairs and knocked on the door bearing the sign, H. L. Dewey, Esquire; Senior Partner. The door was opened and we were greeted by a slightly stooped octogenarian gentleman with a thick head of snow-white hair, a beaming smile and mischievous twinkle in his eye. "Come in. Come in. Sit down. Sit down. Can I get you a coffee, a tea or a soft drink perhaps?" He took his seat behind a grand mahogany double pedestal partner's desk with lion's head brass hardware. The surface of the desk was protected by a brown leather writing surface with burnished copper hand tooling.

We both shook our heads and said in unison, "No, thank you."

"Very well, I always have a coffee around this time. You don't mind do you?" he said lifting the lid of what appeared to be a cigar box but was, in fact, a desk phone. Instantly he was connected to the receptionist. He asked her for his usual morning beverage and turned to us, "Are you certain you won't join me?"

"If you please, Mr. Dewey, how did he die and where is he buried? I'd like to visit his grave."

"I'm sorry, Miss Jewels. I thought you knew."

"Knew what, Mr. Dewey?"

"Why; there was no body. I'm very sorry to inform you. His overturned boat was found floating in the lake and after an exhaustive search he was declared deceased by misadventure." He said.

A heavy silence fell over the room as Heidi digested this unexpected news. "But, how can... I mean there was **no** body. How can someone be declared dead if there's **no body**?"

"Pursuant to section 2 subsection 4 of the Act a Court has the jurisdiction to make an order declaring that an individual has died if the court is satisfied that:

- the individual has disappeared in circumstances of peril;
- the applicant has not heard of or from the individual since the disappearance;
- to the applicant's knowledge, after making reasonable inquiries, no other person has heard of or from the individual since the disappearance;
- the applicant has no reason to believe that the individual is alive; and
- There is sufficient evidence to find that the individual is dead.

I truly am so very sorry, Miss Jewels. I thought you knew. Would you like to take a few moments to gather your thoughts?"

"No. I really must get his estate sorted."

"Before we get down to business I wonder, have you brought anything that can confirm you are who you say you are?" asked the old barrister a little taken aback.

Heidi reached into her backpack and withdrew a sheaf of papers and her EU passport, handing them across the desk, "This is all that I have, sir."

He looked at the passport then over his spectacles at the young woman sitting across the desk from him then again at the passport. Flipping through her papers he found the letter he had sent Heidi's mother then he smiled, "Well, bless my soul. I had given up hope of ever getting to meet LJ's next of kin. You are a sight for sore eyes m' dear and just in time too. The time is up for heirs to come forward tomorrow at noon.

With your permission Miss Jewels, I will begin?"

"Yes, please." Without further ado, he began,

"I HEREBY REVOKE all former wills, codicils and other testamentary dispositions made by me.

I NOMINATE, CONSTITUTE and APPOINT Dewey, Cheetham & Howe, LLB to be the Estate Trustees, Executors, and Trustees of this my Will... (We heard... "blah, blah, blah diddy, blah")

I GIVE, DEVISE, AND BEQUEATH all of my property of every nature and kind and wheresoever situate to my Trustee upon the following trusts, namely:

To pay out of my general estate my debts, funeral and testamentary expenses.

To pay out of my general estate all income taxes, estate, inheritance and succession duties or taxes whether imposed by or pursuant to the law... (Again what we heard was... "blah, blah, blah didy, blah" until we heard...).

In the event that my fourth cousin, Ruby Precious Jewels, shall survive me by a period of thirty (30) days to pay, transfer, and assign the residue of my estate to her for her own use absolutely.

In the event that my fourth cousin, Ruby Precious Jewels, should predecease me I give, devise, and bequeath all of my property of every nature and kind and wheresoever situate to all of the living issue of said cousin per capita. ..."

Mr. Dewey continued at great length for several more minutes but yet again all we heard was, "blah, blah, blah diddy, blah".

I surveyed his office as he spoke. My eyes moved about the room soaking up the ambiance of the warm glow of incandescent lighting on rich mahogany panelled walls. Opposite his desk was a handsome Victorian fireplace carved in a deep red Griotte Rouge marble with large finely carved corbels. Three walls were lined, floor to ceiling, with polished mahogany bookcases displaying an impressive collection of legal tomes.

I absently scanned the room and as my eyes glanced over the analogous collection of books I became aware that a couple of the volumes were not like the others.

My gaze returned to his desk and something that niggled at me but I couldn't quite put my finger on the cause of my misgiving.

"Does that mean that the property is mine, Mr. Dewey?" enquired Heidi nervously.

"Why, yes, yes it does, my dear. I have had all the necessary paperwork drawn up just waiting for the rightful heir to come forward." Buzzing Miss

Onholde he gave her instructions to bring the necessary documents to his office.

"I will see to it that title is registered this afternoon.

I regret it has been necessary to liquidate most of the furnishings to pay final expenses and taxes. I'm afraid all that remains are a lot of old musty books that aren't of much value and I will make arrangements for them to be disposed of for you to recover some of my expenses, you understand. Perhaps the local library might take some or one of the local used bookstores."

"Were you aware that the house had been broken into?" I asked.

"I noticed you've already changed the old locks. Highly irregular in as much as you did not yet have legal title to the property. However, in light of the recent events there, perhaps it was the prudent course of action. Would you be so kind as to let me have a key?"

"Why, yes. I have an extra key right here." Heidi replied rummaging in her backpack.

My attention returned once more to his very elegant desk and a catalogue resting on the corner.

"If you'll just excuse me a moment I'll just take the file to my secretary to begin the registration process. Would you care for a celebratory beverage while you wait? A coffee or tea perchance?" Proposed the jovial old solicitor.

Again we declined and Mr. Dewey left his office file in hand to set legal wheels in motion, as it were.

The moment he was out of the room I said quietly to Heidi, "When he comes back ask him for an inventory of the furnishings he has sold."

"Why?"

"I think there's something dodgy about Mr. Dewey and his handling of the estate."

"But he seems so nice and besides he was a friend of my grandfather's?"

"Just humour me," I whispered.

Getting up from my chair I took a closer look at two books that stood out from the others on the shelf. One was "In Our Time" by Ernest Hemingway and the other was "Tamerlane and Other Poems" by Edgar Allan Poe.

Stepping around his desk I read the cover, The Antiquarian, and leafed through a few pages. It was a catalogue of rare books just a few days old, he was a bibliophile. He had bookmarked certain pages and turning to the first bookmarked page I was taken aback to see a first edition of The Adventures of Huckleberry Finn by Mark Twain and signed by the author listed at $53,415. I turned to another flagged page and was gobsmacked to see Alice's Adventures in Wonderland by Lewis Carroll with a price tag of $3,000,000.

I could hear his approaching footsteps in the hall and returned quickly to my chair. I nudged Heidi and whispered, "Don't give him a key. I'll explain later."

"Well now, everything is in motion." He said smiling and looking at his desk. "Were you able to locate a key?"

"Would it be possible to get a copy of an inventory of the contents of the estate including what they were sold for and a statement of expenses paid?"

"Certainly, Miss Jewels. I'll have Levinia include a copy with your documents and you can pick them up on your way out."

"Thank you very kindly, Mr. Dewey, but I have a passion for reading and I'd love to browse the shelves, myself."

"Oh, um, er..." He stammered as he thought feverishly for a plausible line of reasoning as to why he should be allowed to clear the library shelves. Failing in his endeavour he replied, "Well, if you're absolutely, certain this is what you want Miss Jewels. I guess I can wait a little longer for my fee.

How can I get hold of you if I need to?"

"Mr. Case's parents have kindly offered to let me stay with them until I can make my house habitable. I'll leave their phone number with your secretary."

"Yes, yes, very well, Miss Jewels."

"Thank you for all you've done," Heidi said standing to leave.

"My pleasure, Miss Jewels, my pleasure indeed. LJ and I have been friends for many years. If I may be of any further service don't hesitate to get in touch with our office." He said smiling uncertainly as if trying to fathom why Heidi had changed her mind and what he might do to persuade her to let him have the books as we left his office.

Out in the car I described to Heidi what I had observed on the Barrister's bookshelves and in the catalogue. "We need to get copies of antique furniture and rare book catalogues from somewhere and go through the inventory and all of the books on your shelves.

Read the riddle again."

"Why?" she asked, perplexed.

"Indulge me," I said.

Heidi, a puzzled look on her face, took out the dog-eared sheet, unfolded it and read,

"The gold, how it shone
right where you left it, gone.
Waiting for the light
hidden in plain sight.
No longer gold
Many stories are told."

"I think the second line clearly, tells us the gold is no longer where it was first buried. I also think the fifth line tells us that the gold has been converted into another asset of equal value and is hidden in plain sight only concealed by darkness."

"But why didn't you want me to let Mr. Dewey clear out the old books?" she asked.

"I think the last line tells us why Mr. Dewey is so anxious to get his hands on your books; 'Many stories told' refers to your books. The catalogue on his desk was The Antiquarian, a catalogue of rare books and he had bookmarked several of the books I saw on your bookshelves. There was a first edition of Atlas Shrugged with a price tag of $42,732, The Adventures of Huckleberry Finn by Mark Twain signed by the author listed at $53,415 and others.

I think one of your ancestors found the treasure and hid it in plain sight by using the gold to purchase rare and valuable books and furniture. I also think that whether Dewey realized this or not he did recognize that what was on the bookshelves of your house is worth a fortune.

I have my suspicions about the accuracy of Mr. Dewey's inventory. That, however, will be much more difficult to prove and take a lot of time and leg work." Heidi sat open-mouthed as I started the engine, backed the car out of the parking spot and headed for her house.

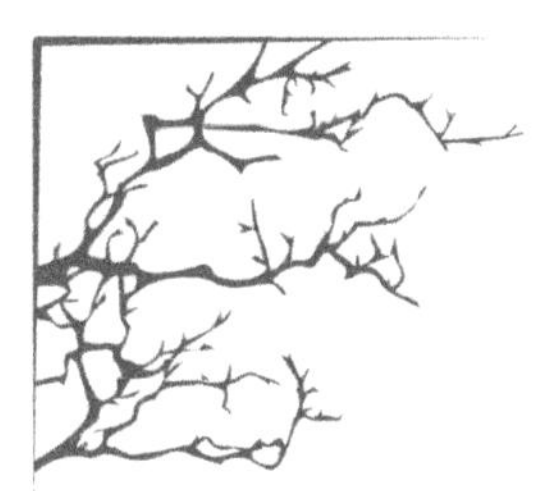

6 Let there be light

First, we visited the library to borrow copies of The Antiquarian rare book catalogue and the 1stDIBS antique furniture catalogue. Next, we visited a drive-through to pick up lunch before driving out to Heidi's new home. We travelled in companionable silence, each with thoughts of adventure and discovery.

I had brought a hammer, cordless drill, crowbar and ladder with me and upon arriving got right to work removing the boards from the sitting room windows. The boards were held in place by screws and were quickly and easily unfastened with my cordless drill and once removed the shutters were opened and the sitting room was filled with light. Heidi opened the windows allowing a soft breeze to fill the room.

My curiosity burning I picked up The Antiquarian and flipped through to the page exhibiting, "In Our Time" by Ernest Hemingway. The price under the image of the book was $321,600. I then turned to the page displaying an image of, "Tamerlane and Other Poems" by Edgar Allan Poe the price of which was $662,500.

"You've got to see this, Heidi," I said holding the catalogue out.

"Those books were on the Barrister's bookshelf. I think our Mr. Dewey has been helping himself to the cookie jar."

"Why that... What am I going to do?"

"You need to have proof of his misappropriation before you can take action. He'll have a second set of books for the estate assets he's sold. We need to get a look at those books."

"But how? He's not going to just hand them over." she whinged.

"I don't know yet," I said thoughtfully. "First, let's take a look at the books you have. Perhaps you can sell a couple to get yourself set up."

Heidi would be busy over the next few days setting up accounts with the various utilities but for now the light flooding in illuminated the bookshelves adequately. We began taking books off of the shelves and looking them over carefully then researching them in the catalogue we had gotten at the library. In no time we found Atlas Shrugged, The Adventures of Huckleberry Finn, Treasure Island, The Grapes of Wrath, John Milton's Paradise Lost and James Joyce's Kent, on just one shelf, for a total value of $238,635.

Heidi was so excited she could scarcely contain herself and at the same time confused and furious over the betrayal by an old friend of L. John Silver III and a solicitor with a fiduciary duty to serve their client.

The crunch of tires on gravel in the driveway could be heard causing us to go to the window. The guys had arrived in Lawson's truck and brought their tools to get to work.

Lawson, Nack, Nick, Moose and Hugo piled out of the truck and I set about making introductions. I was gobsmacked as Hugo immediately began flirting with Heidi who seemed charmed by his attention. I was rankled that Hugo would do this and that the time Heidi and I had spent together apparently meant nothing to her and it irritated me that that irritated me.

We all went into the sitting room where I told the guys about Heidi's meeting with Mr. Hugh Dewey and how I had discovered the treasure. "She'll have enough money to preserve her heritage and live here comfortably."

Lawson, always eager to get things done, spoke up, "Pitter patter let's get at 'er. First things first; we've got a tree blocking the drive." We had the tree limbed, cut up into fireplace size pieces and stacked ready for winter.

After a brief break and brown pop each Lawson, not one to sit around when there was work to be done proclaimed, "We're burnin' daylight. We need to get the boards of these windows so we can see what we're doing."

A couple of hours later and all of the boards had been removed from the windows and shutters were opened. The light began to fade and our stomachs began to grumble. Lawson motioned to me to go to the truck with him. He had thoughtfully loaded a barbeque, charcoal, utensils and two coolers, one with steaks and fresh corn on the cob and one with ice-cold beverages. "Wow, Lawson! You think of everything. Thanks."

After Lawson, Nack, Nick, Moose and I each cracked a cold one Lawson put the steaks on the barbeque.

Nack and Nick kept Lawson company while he played chef. Moose and I settled back to look over the inventory Mr. Dewey had provided. We compared the inventory of furnishings he had sold to pay expenses with the few similar listings we could find in the 1stDIBS antique furniture catalogue. "At first glance, it appeared that the inventory values, suspiciously, do not match the catalogue values of similar pieces. This is going to take some time. We will have to find and visit each of the purchasers of the furnishings and then have the stuff appraised." Advised Moose.

After stuffing my face with a couple of hamburgers I ventured inside to look over the bookshelves again. My OCD senses were tingling and that's when I noticed what appeared to be an anomaly. Among the books on the bottom shelf, one book was upside down. 'I wouldn't be so OCD if everyone else just did things right.' I thought to myself. I should explain that I have a mild case of obsessive-compulsive disorder. I even rotate the dishes in my cupboard so the bottom ones don't feel left out and the same with many other things.

The offending book that had attracted my attention was, "Hunting for Hidden Gold", a Hardy Boys adventure. It had been improperly positioned on the shelf and begged to be put right. Unable to stop myself I took it from the shelf to replace it properly. A few pages protruded irksomely. Opening the book to straighten them I discovered they were folded loose-leaf pages containing some sort of lists.

I couldn't believe what I was seeing. I had stumbled upon the original inventory of the furnishings of the house and an inventory of the books in the house's library made by their owner, Longue John Silver III.

Just then Moose and Nick entered the room. "What're you up to in here?" asked Lawson.

"You'll never guess what I found."

"What did you find?" asked Nick.

I showed my two friends what I had discovered.

Moose took the pages from my hand and after scanning them said, "We've got the proof of embezzlement right here."

Nick asked excitedly, "Hey, where's Hugo and Heidi? Shouldn't we show her what you've found?"

"I seen them heading for the beach a few minutes ago," said Nack who had just joined us.

"I seen them..." was like fingernails on a blackboard and to add insult to injury, Hugo had swept Heidi away. Even though it had seemed inevitable I still felt the sting of resentment.

Our conversation turned to Heidi's library and the treasure concealed within. "There's every reason to believe that Dewey will attempt to procure, at least some of the most valuable books in the collection.

The body that was found upstairs means there's someone out there that isn't afraid to kill to keep a secret. Which reminds me, I wonder if DSS Kaye has returned the key to the old bat in the Registry Office, not that it makes a great deal of difference now." I said. That nagging feeling had returned that, besides the obvious, something wasn't right. "Body, drug lab, keys, signs then like a blinding flash of light in the darkness I saw it. The only one that knew I was going to 1758 Sleepy Hollow Lane was Mrs. Eileen Wright at the Prince Edward County Land Registry Office."

"Ya, and don't forget the Hopper brothers." Added Nick.

"We need a plan." Offered Moose, who was already formulating one.

"We could... No, he'd see that coming. Maybe we could set a trap?

Hey, Justin. What are you suggesting?" queried Nack. "Justin, are you listening?"

"I need to call DSS Kaye as soon as possible," I said. "I think all or some of us need to stay here tonight.

Heidi needs to snap herself out of her state of Twitterpation and make some decisions fast. She needs to take her books out of play by making the collection a matter of public record. She needs to get an expert in to inventory the collected works and she needs to insure the collection."

"I've got to go to work. I took today off, I can't take another." Nick put in.

Lawson said, "You take my truck back to town and we'll come back to town with Justin tomorrow."

"You guys'll have to sort it out; right now I have to get to a phone," I said as I headed for my car.

I drove around to 1758 Sleepy Hollow Lane in the hopes that I might find DSS Kaye or DS Nyne there. I thought that if neither were there an officer would be on duty and could get word to them. Pulling into the driveway Sergeant Kent B. Goode exited the front door and came striding towards the car.

"I'm sorry sir but this is a crime scene, oh, it's you, Mr. Case. How are you and what brings you here?" said the big man.

"Hello, Sergeant. I don't suppose DSS Kaye or DS Nyne would be around, by any chance? I need to speak with them urgently."

"No, sir, they're back at headquarters. May I be of any help?" rumbled Goode.

"Can you get a message to DSS Kaye? I think I know who switched the signs. And stop calling me sir. My name is Justin, Sergeant." I urged.

"Why, yes sir. I'll radio him for you right away."

Within a few minutes, Sergeant Goode had DSS Kaye on the line. "Here you are, sir."

"Good evening, Mr. Case. What can I do for you?" the irritated voice of DSS Kaye came over the police radio.

I told Kaye about Heidi's meeting with Hugh Dewey. I explained about his being a bibliophile and seeing the catalogue on his desk and the books Heidi had inherited. I even mentioned the Hopper brothers' appearance at the old house.

"I'm afraid there's nothing illegal about being a bibliophile, Mr. Case, so I fail to see why you think any of this would be of the slightest interest to me. You are wasting police time." He said impatiently.

"Yes, but what about, "In Our Time" by Ernest Hemingway worth $321,600 and the other book "Tamerlane and Other Poems" by Edgar Allan Poe valued at $662,500, the books I saw on his bookshelves? Surely that's got to be suspicious?" I wheedled.

"That's certainly a great deal of money but can you prove those books belonged to the estate, Mr. Case?" he said irritably.

"Well, no, but..." I groused.

I had thought that Kaye being a detective could have put two and two together. "Well, I got to thinking about the body in the chair and then I wondered if you had returned the key to the Registry Office. That's when it dawned on me; Eileen Wright from the Prince Edward County Registry Office was the only one that knew I was going to 1758 Sleepy Hollow Lane. I think she must have contacted someone at the drug lab to warn them and they switched the signs."

To my great surprise, his tone had lost its irritation and he was unusually voluble. "Very imaginative of you Mr. Case. Our routine investigation found nothing to connect her with the lab but perhaps another look wouldn't hurt."

"Have you caught the people responsible for the drug lab? Am I in danger?"

"No, we haven't apprehended the offenders and probably never will. The house was leased to an offshore corporation with no listed officers or owners. The house itself had been sanitized.

There's no reason to think they would risk coming after you, Mr. Case." He sounded tired and perhaps a little defeated.

"Have you identified the person in the chair? How did they die? I didn't see any blood. Was it poison?"

At this, his tone was filled with sadness. "You'll read about this in the papers anyway. His name was Sergeant Lou Tenant an RCMP undercover narcotics agent. He was stabbed with a thin, needle-like weapon about six inches long. The doctor said there wouldn't have been much pain and he would have died from internal bleeding within a few minutes."

"I'm so sorry for your loss, Detective Staff Sergeant Kaye. Did he have a family?"

"Being a cop is hard enough on family life but going undercover makes having a family not only dangerous but next to impossible.

Was there anything else, Mr. Case?"

"No, thank you, you've been most helpful and patient. Again, my condolences. Good night, Detective Staff Sergeant Kaye."

"Good night, Mr. Case."

7 a bent barrister takes the bait

We didn't get much sleep in the cold, damp and very noisy edifice. The creaking and groaning of the old house kept us alert and straining for even the slightest sound of someone approaching. We couldn't light a fire in the ancient fireplace for fear the light would be seen by our expected visitor. We sat on the cold, hard floor of the sitting room with our backs to the wall, listening.

Suddenly the beams from car headlights swept across the room and then I heard the faint sound of tires on gravel as a car pulled to a stop out front. I had hidden my car out of sight in the old carriage house around the back. Moose's strategy was about to play out.

Notcho's low rumbling growl seemed to vibrate the air around us. "Shsh," I whispered trying to keep her quiet.

Moose nudged Lawson who had managed, somehow, to fall asleep. "Our guest has arrived," he whispered.

Moose and I got quietly to our feet followed groggily by Lawson. We moved soundlessly to a place of concealment.

Nack, Hugo, and Heidi were already out of sight in the dining room.

Scratching and clicking noises emanated from the big oak doors as someone jimmied the new lock. "If he damages that new lock he'll regret it." Muttered Lawson, under his breath as a frigid blast of air enveloped us as the mysterious caller slowly opened the big front door.

We watched as the shaft of light from a flashlight played across the foyer and then into the study. The shaft of light began scanning the bookcases as if looking for a favourite book. It finally came to rest on the First Edition of Alice's Adventures in Wonderland by Lewis Carroll valued at Two to Three Million Dollars.

I readied my Brownie Starmite II camera and checked the peanut flash bulb to make sure it was seated securely.

A floorboard creaked somewhere in the darkness of the old house. The figure froze listening and looked over its shoulder nervously. Then, after what seemed an eternity, the thief appeared satisfied they were alone and returned to their nefarious endeavour. Slowly they reached out to gingerly take hold of the object of their desire.

It was at that moment that chaos erupted. Notcho strained against my grip, her claws scrabbling on the floor trying to gain traction. I released my hold as my flash went off, its brilliance momentarily blinding everyone and illuminating Mr. Dewey with an outstretched hand holding the purloined publication.

Something hurtled from the shadows. The unseen creature landed with a shriek on the miscreant's back its fists flailing.

Meanwhile, Notcho had clamped her teeth onto the intruder's leg. Her muffled growls could just be heard amid the mêlée.

Suddenly the beams of five flashlights converged on them. "Help! Get them off of me!" The would-be thief wailed.

Hugo, who was close on her heels, grabbed hold of the wildly thrashing Heidi, "Okay, Heidi. We've got him."

I took hold of Notcho and pulled her off still snarling.

"You... you swindler!" she shouted at him.

"Oh! What in blazes! Who...but I thought..." spluttered a surprised Mr. Dewey.

"Looking for a little light reading, perhaps, Mr. Dewey? Alice's Adventures in Wonderland by Lewis Carroll, you have excellent taste in reading material, I must say. That one will set you back about $3,000,000. Would you care to explain yourself?" I asked.

"You stole from Long John. He thought you were his friend. He trusted you." Complained a clearly, irate Heidi, being restrained by Hugo.

Beads of sweat broke out on his forehead and his face was drained of its colour as he stammered, "I thought the house would be empty. How did you know?" looking pathetically from Heidi to me and then he sunk to the floor.

Sniffing and adjusting his glasses Moose said, "The police are on their way, Mr. Dewey.

Justin found the original inventories so there's no use denying your fraud."

Red and blue lights seemed to swirl throughout the room painting the walls with dazzling colours announcing the arrival of the cavalry. Car doors slammed as officers piled out of vehicles. The heavy footfalls of boots could be heard echoing in the empty hall as several police officers led by Detective Staff Sergeant Oxley Kaye and Detective Sergeant Beck Nyne entered the room.

"Everyone, hands where we can see them. Don't move; any of you." O' Kaye bellowed as his officers placed us all in secure positions against the walls.

"Officer, my name is Hugh Louis Dewey, Esquire, Barrister and senior partner at Dewey, Cheetham & Howe. I was just checking the estate for intruders and vandals when these people attacked me and held me against my will." Protested Mr. Dewey.

"Yes, yes. We'll get to you in a moment, Mr. Dewey."

"I want to charge that little hooligan with assault. Where are you going? You've got to listen to me."

"Detective Sergeant Nyne read Mr. Dewey his rights and escort him out to a squad car."

"Yes sir."

"Bu... but... I couldn't stop myself." stammered Mr. Dewey as he began to sob. "Don't you see? She's never... She'd never appreciate... I needed the money. I'll be ruined." He begged.

Ignoring Mr. Dewey's pleas he said, "Now, would someone please explain what's been going on here?"

Moose opened his mouth to speak but was stopped short when Kaye held up his hand and said, "I'll get to you in a moment, sir."

Everyone turned and looked at me so I explained, "I've already told you about my suspicions but without tangible proof, you weren't able to help us.

Heidi just happened to mention to Mr. Dewey that she would be spending the night at my place which meant that no one would be in the house. We thought he would figure this would be his last chance to help himself to the treasure."

Meanwhile, forensics fingerprinted everyone and dusted the front door and library for prints and photographed the front door lock for evidence it was jimmied.

"What were you playing at putting yourselves in harm's way? One or all of you could have been injured or worse." An infuriated Kaye admonished us. "Treasure, what this about a treasure?" asked Kaye, perplexed.

I handed him the dog-eared copy of Picturesque Prince Edward County by Himmler Renell, 1890 open to page 42, "A Cask of Gold" by H. C. Widdowfield. Then I nodded to Heidi who handed him the poetic riddle.

"What's this then?" he said as read the poem:

The gold, how it shone
right where you left it, gone.
Waiting for the light
hidden in plain sight.
No longer gold
Many stories are told.

"The second line "right where you left it gone." means it's no longer where it was buried. And, "hidden in plain sight" suggests it can be seen if we look in the right place. This old house seemed like the logical place to start. The fifth line tells us that the gold has been converted into another form of asset of equal value.

What better form of an asset than furnishings and books?

Unfortunately, Mr. Dewey had a head start on me in figuring this out and had already begun to plunder the estate."

"How very astute of you, Mr. Case."

"Oh, and I was able to snap a picture of Mr. Dewey in the act of removing a rare book from Miss Jewels' library and he jimmied the lock to get in."

"How did you know it was Dewey that was stealing the books and that he would show up?" asked the curious cop.

"When we visited his office I recognized "In Our Time" by Ernest Hemingway and "Tamerlane and Other Poems" by Edgar Allan Poe on his bookshelves. They are worth $321,600 and $662,500 respectively.

I didn't know for sure he would risk a final attempt but we needed solid evidence of his guilt and I thought Alice's Adventures in Wonderland by Lewis Carroll with a price tag of $3,000,000 would be too much for him to pass up. It was worth a shot."

"How do you know they are from the estate?"

"They are both listed in the original inventory but not on the inventory he had given Heidi. This was further proof of his embezzlement and theft of items from the estate of Mr. Long John Silver III."

Moose handed him copies of the original inventories and the fraudulent inventories Dewey had given Heidi. "I believe Mr. Dewey would have kept a second set of books." Offered Moose.

Kaye looked brooding as he said, "We'll need formal statements from everyone. Tomorrow will be soon enough. DS Nyne will arrange a time for you to come to the station. Oh, and I'll need that film." He said holding his hand out expectantly. "That will be all for now. We'll take it from here."

"One more thing Detective?"

"Oh, what's that, Mr. Case?"

"About the body in the locked room upstairs; I think I know how the murderer made their escape."

"And just how do you think they did it, Mr. Case?" he said cynically emphasizing my name disparagingly.

"I'll show you," I said climbing the stairs, followed by everyone,

Arriving at the bedroom across the hall from the scene of the murder I took the key from the door of the room in question.

I then took a length of string, from my pocket and tied it to the key around the throating just behind the bit. Next, I threaded the string through the keyhole from the inside then I closed and locked the door. Placing the key on the floor beneath the door I slowly pulled the string until the key seated itself in the keyhole on the inside of the door. Finally, I struck a match and lit the string close to the latch and watched as the string burned leaving nothing but a minute trace of ash and the whiff of burnt string.

A look of astonishment on his face as he said, "A very entertaining parlour trick, Mr. Case but we can't prove that was how it was done."

"Oh, but I think we can. That's why I used this door for the demonstration and not the crime scene door. Ask your forensic team to check the keyhole for string fibres and evidence of burnt string in the lock."

"NYNE!" he yelled.

Nyne could be heard scrambling across the foyer and up the stairs two at a time. "Sir?"

"Get forensics up here; NOW!"

"Sir."

A few minutes later forensics confirmed the presence of string fibres and traces of ash in the lock.

Kaye was right, that was just a parlour trick. I was still troubled by what I couldn't explain. "What was that police officer in the rocking chair doing in the house? Who murdered him and why?" I asked out loud.

Kaye just looked at me and shook his head gloomily.

The bedlam was over and.

The next morning, bright and early, we met for coffee and then drove to the police station for our interviews.

A month later my band of brothers from other mothers and I visited Heidi for a BBQ and to catch up. She had sold a couple of books to the Thomas Fisher Rare Book Library, the largest repository of publically accessible rare books and manuscripts in Canada which allowed her to take care of a few structural issues and furnish the house. Heidi had begun her new life.

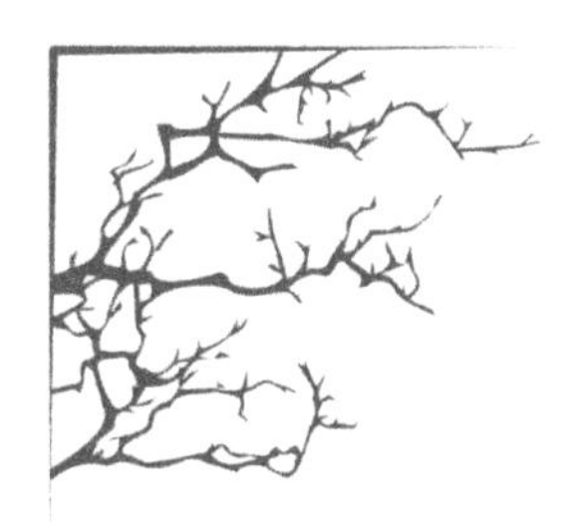

Vanished

The second of three adventures in the trilogy of Chasing the Wendigo as told by

Justin Case

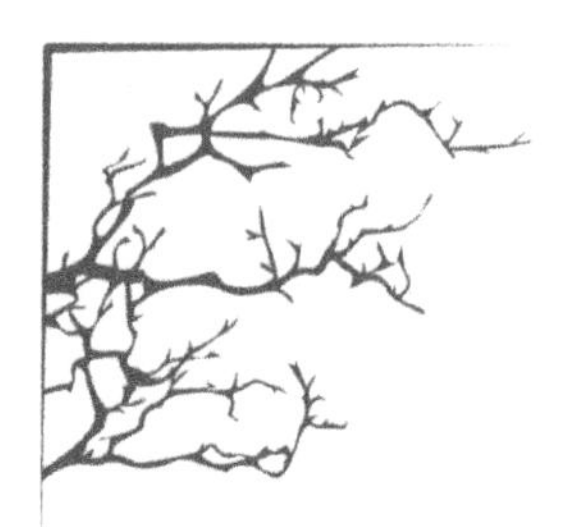

DEDICATION

His last words were, "I'm off, see you tonight". Never to be seen or heard from again.
Families of missing people are often understood as inhabiting a particular space of ambiguity, captured in the phrase, "living in limbo".
Most of us in well-resourced, democratic societies live with taken-for-granted securities in ordinary life in which our living loved ones are almost always contactable or known to be *somewhere*. For some, however, this sense of security is threatened when a family member or friend or colleague is missing, something that happens with surprising frequency with 73,620 incidents in Canada in 2018 alone.
This story is dedicated to all those left behind and those that search for the *VANISHED.*

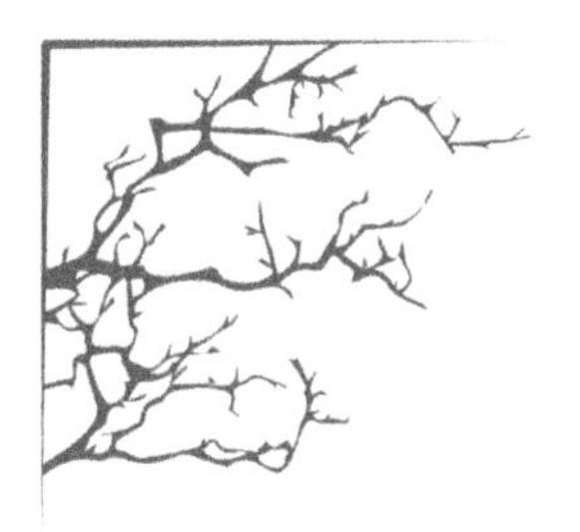

1 Without a Trace

Throughout history there have been numerous cases of people who have simply vanished without a trace, disappearing forever without explanation or resolution. This is certainly spooky enough when it's just one person, but it becomes decidedly more bizarre when large groups of people abruptly cease to exist, never to be seen again. Indeed, some of the most baffling disappearances in history involve the mass purging of entire communities. What unseen malevolent forces are responsible for these inexplicable incidents? We may never know.

The Roanoke colony was established in 1587 on Roanoke Island, today known as North Carolina, by settlers from England. John White, the governor of the colony, returned from a supply trip to Europe only to find that the entire settlement had been deserted. All that remained was a skeleton and the word "Croatoan" etched into a tree.

The Mary Celeste set sail from New York bound for Genoa, Italy in 1872. She was found, not a soul aboard, drifting aimlessly in the Atlantic Ocean about 740 kilometres off the coast of the Azores, her entire cargo and supplies untouched. Strangely the Captain's logbook that should have been taken by the crew even in the event of abandoning ship remained.

On October 3, 1955, the merchant vessel MV Joyita departed Samoa, with 25 souls aboard, for the Tokelau Islands. A month later, she was found drifting in the South Pacific, 600 miles off her course. All passengers, crew and cargo had vanished baffling investigators.

In February 1923, the 600 residents of the small Brazilian village of Hoer Verde simply vanished, leaving all their possessions and food behind. Visitors to the village were struck by the deathly silence. Police were summoned from a nearby town. They went from building to building looking for any sign of life without success. However, upon entering the village school house they found a gun recently fired and a cryptic message scrawled on the blackboard, "There is no salvation."

No trace of the 600 villagers of Hoer Verde has ever been unearthed.

On the southernmost region of Alaska's Kenai Peninsula lie the remnants of a small village called Portlock. The town began in the early 1900s as a cannery for salmon. In the 1920s, Albert Petka reported running off a peculiar animal with his dogs before receiving a fatal blow from the creature. Ten years later, a piece of logging equipment hit a logger in the head, even though it would have taken more than one person to lift it. The logger died, and the unusual trend continued when several hunters disappeared a few years later. Their bodies floated in with the morning tide. Something had partially dismembered and beaten them. Over 20 years, people claimed to find more than 30 bodies in the same state.

In the 1940s, there were rumours of disappearances and murders and the discovery of giant footprints, and sightings of a mysterious beast.

In the far north of Canada,

Lake Anjikuni can be an inhospitable place. Several villages existed along the shores of the lakes, home to the Inuit and a welcome resting point for the fur trappers who braved the far north to hunt beaver and caribou. But something happened to one of the villages in 1930 which remains a mystery to this day.

A news reporter in The Pas, Manitoba, Emmett Kelleher, reported about a small Inuit community off the coast of Lake Anjikuni on November 29, 1930. According to the story Joe Labelle, a well-known fur trapper, discovered an empty camp with six tents, but of the 25 men, women, and children who lived there, there was no sign.

During his search, he discovered incomplete garments with needles still in them, as well as food hung over fire pits, but no traces of violence or a conflict that would have explained the people's absence.

Moving through the village, Labelle found seven sled dogs still tied to their posts: they had all starved to death. These dogs would have been vital to the survival of the community and to leave them behind would have been almost unthinkable.

But then, on the edge of the village, Labelle found something even more chilling. A human grave had been recently dug up. Because the stones encircling the burial were undisturbed, Labelle recognized it couldn't have been an animal. A human had done this.

Could these mysterious disappearances have been the work of a Wendigo?

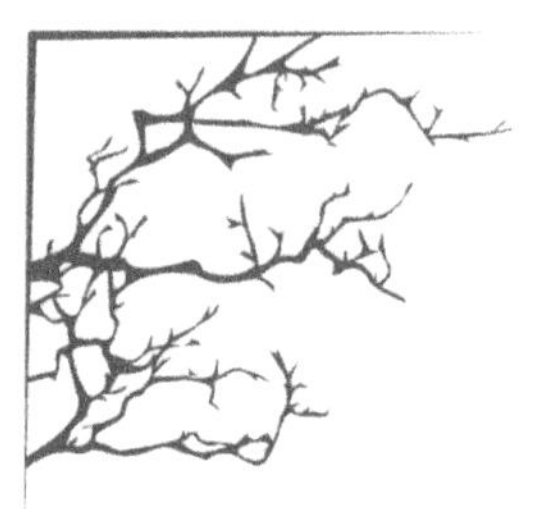

2 friends & family

Friday night found us all at the Break & Run Pool Hall. All, that is, except for, Nack's twin brother, Nick. The twins were fit, good-looking men of Italian and Nordic descent with quiet, unassuming demeanours. The room was filled with the familiar clacking, clicking and rolling sounds of pool balls on felt. Amid the murmur of conversation as opponents selected their implements of convivial combat were the sounds of balls being racked, the squeak of chalk being applied to cue tips, the gentle thud of cue tips striking cue balls and the clack of the cue balls caroming off their targets. There was also the disappointing sound of a cue ball inadvertently missing its intended target, thumping softly off of the rubber rail, and dropping with a strangely satisfying yet disappointing clunk into the unintended pocket.

Nick, you remember Nick? A string erector for the Tin Can Communications or TCC Company and twin brother of Nack, a tin can installer with a background in chemical technology. The following is the curious chronicle communicated to Nack, Hugo, Moose, Lawson and me by Nick one night in a pub over a few brown pops.

Well, Nick had been sent to work installing poles and running line to the remote settlement of Thelost, set unobtrusively on the shores of Gonemissing Lake, not too far from the northernmost reaches of Allegory Park.

Nick was running late because of the long drive from The Last Resort that the TCC had billeted him in, that, although the closest to Thelost Village, 36 minutes or 31.4 kilometres, was 428 kilometres or 4 hours 21 minutes to his home in Bonnechance.

He had left work early astride his Triumph and ridden like a man possessed, frustration and exasperation burning within him. The TCC had agreed to send a two-man line crew on this remote job and yet here he was on his own. The Association had repeatedly pressed their case of the dangers of one-man line crews, especially in remote areas.

The air streaming in his face was bracing, the throb of the high-performance motor and the sensation of becoming one with his machine created a meditative state calming his agitation. The wind would soon become bitter and bone-chilling as summer turned to fall. Sadly it would soon be time to put his bike up for the winter and take his Camero. He would contact his manager on Monday and insist on someone to join him on the line.

He decided to think about something else. It was time to finalize plans for a winter getaway with Justin. He was looking forward to a week in Freeport, on Grand Bahamas Island. The resort spanned the island offering two beaches and boasting twenty-seven holes of golf. A meeting with the travel agent was set for tomorrow to give her their deposit.

Finally reaching Bonnechance Nick stopped first at his family home where delicious and steaming hot spaghetti and stewed pork heart awaited him. He put Gordie Lightfoot on the record player and helped himself to a heaping plate of his favourite comfort food. Afterwards, he washed, dressed and climbed into his Camero setting out for the Break & Run Pool Hall.

"Well, look at what the cat dragged in," greeted Moose, as Nick came through the door.

Everyone's heads turned.

"Hi, Moose," he responded affably.

"Ya, if it isn't the late Nick Tchotchke," sniggered a patently athletic, freckle-faced young man with thinning, reddish brown hair. He sported a moustache and a barely noticeable scar acquired when a nasty piece of work tried to decapitate him, but that's a story for another day. Hugo leaned over the table racking up the balls.

"Ya, long time, no see," said Nick.

After hearty greetings all around, we got down to a friendly game of sticks and balls.

"Are we still on for tomorrow morning at 10:00?" Nick asked me.

"You bet; I'll meet you there. How was your ride down?" I asked.

Before Nick could respond, "Who's gonna break?" urged Hugo trying to hurry things along.

"I'll break," offered Moose, with the customary curl of his upper lip and sniff, as he stepped up to the table and positioned the cue ball. He took aim and his cue made the familiar soft tonk as it contacted the white sphere. He sent the cue ball, at speed, between the brown and yellow balls and passed the triangle of fifteen red balls with a pink ball at its apex, rebounding with a thump from the bumper narrowly missing the black ball and striking the waiting triangle of red balls from behind with a resounding clack. This manoeuvre sent the red balls gently caroming in all directions but cleverly left the cue ball tucked tactically and safely in a cluster of red balls.

"I'm snookered. Thanks a lot, Moose. I thought this was a friendly game." I chided affably.

This started Moose off. "The origin of snooker balls, as well as billiards, is a fascinating tale of mystery."

Moose adjusted his glasses, curled his lip and sniffed, settling into his subject, "Did you know that wood was originally used to make the balls? However, although popular through the 16th century the exquisitely made balls were prone to warping.

Unfortunately, in the 17th century, their searches for a more suitable medium for pool balls lead them to ivory. Regrettably, the global popularity of ivory balls meant that elephants were hunted to the point of extinction in the middle to late 18th century.

Luckily, John Wesley Hyatt came to the rescue of the elephant. The development of the nitrocellulose compound replaced the ivory billiard and snooker balls in 1869.

There was, however, one small problem with the new balls. They would explode if struck with too much force. The exploding balls were understandably discontinued.

The next incarnation of the balls was Bakelite and phenolic resin allowing for high-precision spheres with high-quality finishes. More importantly and of great relief to the players, they didn't explode." He concluded just in time for his shot.

While Nack and Nick waited patiently for Moose to finish, I heard Nack quietly ask his brother, "How's work? Who did they send up with you?" Nack sounded as if he was making an effort to keep the concern out of his voice.

Nick, leaning on his cue and looking very serious, responded gloomily, "They didn't send anybody. I'm by myself on the line."

Lawson overheard Nick and stuck his oar in, "That's a dangerous practice. What happens if you're injured or your truck rolls over?"

"Ya, I'm going to speak with the Association Rep on Monday and put in a grievance," muttered Nick irritably.

"You mean, Enzo Watt?" asked Lawson.

"Ya, I'm meeting with him after I meet with the shop foreperson, Laura Deboom."

"Don't corner something meaner than you," Lawson teased.

"It's your shot" prompted Moose.

It wasn't long before we had had enough pool and Hugo asked, "B & F or Holin Wah?"

We agreed on Chinese, paid our bill at the Break & Run and made our way to the restaurant. The conversation soon turned to the mysterious village of Thelost.

"Are they friendly?" I asked.

"Ya, they seem normal. Everyone seemed busy with chores when I was there. I haven't really, been to the village much. I met with their leader, Zeke Himphurst, when I first got there, to let him know we were installing the lines. Other than that I've been swamped trying to set poles and run lines." Nick replied.

"How are the bugs back there? I hear the mosquitoes are the size of birds and black flies blot out the sun." I chuckled.

"Ya, Justin, you need to beat them off with a baseball bat," Nick said with a quiet laugh.

"I've heard they grow wacky tobaccy and other weird stuff," said Moose.

Hugo sniggered.

"I wouldn't know, Moose, I haven't seen any but they offered me some vegetables from their gardens and fresh eggs from their chickens." This seemed to have satiated everyone's curiosity for the moment and our conversation turned to golf. We ate too much had a few laughs and then trekked off to our respective homes for the night. The talk of Thelost Village had piqued my curiosity.

Saturday morning I spent a couple of hours washing, waxing and vacuuming my pride and joy, a metallic blue Mustang before I was to be at the travel agent's with Nick. My mind wandered, as I worked, back to the conversation of last night about the Thelost Village, on the shore of Gonemissing Lake and shrouded in mystery where Nick had been sent to install tin can (phone) poles and lines. Who were these people? Where had they come from?

Something clinked as it was sucked up by the vacuum. It was a slightly different sound than the gravel made as it passed along the vacuum wand. I thought no more of it until I was emptying the bag and noticed the glint of something glossy pink in the dirt; a false fingernail. "That's odd. I wonder where that came from." I absently put it in my pocket in case I found its owner.

My thoughts wandered, as they do, and I thought of the dead RCMP undercover narcotics officer. He must have been discovered by the miscreants responsible for the drugs lab on Sleepy Hollow Lane and the nasty, Mrs. Eileen Wright. I was sure she was involved.

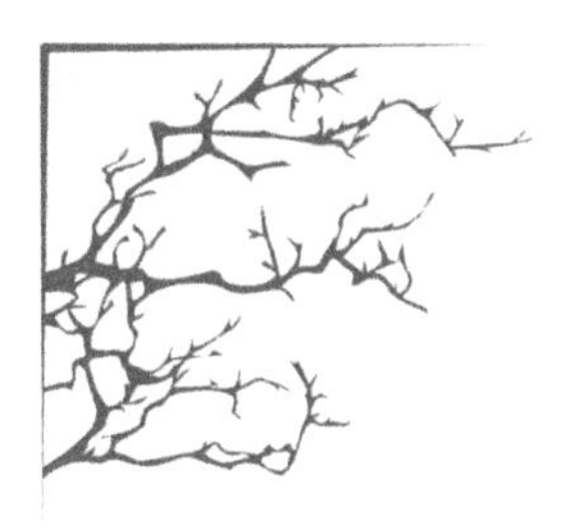

3 gathering storm

Sinister myths and legends of its mysterious origins swirl around the Thelost Village that seemed to have simply sprung up. No one knows when the first settlers arrived or where they came from.

One such rumour suggested that these were the missing villagers of the Inuit fishing village on Nunavut's Angikuni Lake. However, the inhabitants of Thelost did not appear to be of the Inuit race.

Someone suggested they were an alien colony, one of many around the world.

The enigmatic residents of Thelost Village were self-sufficient only venturing into town when absolutely, necessary such as when they had a surplus to trade or sell. During these visits, their strange appearance drew furtive sidelong glances and whispers. All of the settlers wore hand-knit wool hats. The men were dressed in knitted wool shirts with felt pants and the women knitted wool tops and felt skirts. On their feet, they wore woven birch bark shoes lined with cattail down and willow bark soles. Some residents even crossed to the opposite side of the street when they saw them, out of a baseless fear of the unknown.

Nick, being of a jovial nature got to know a few of the inhabitants of Thelost and found them friendly and shy. In fact, upon arriving at his job site each, and every morning he found two warm buttermilk biscuits with plenty of fresh, rich, and hand-churned butter and two hard-boiled eggs waiting for him. Moreover, on a couple of very hot days, he had looked down from the top of a pole to see three or four children and a beautiful young woman leaving a jug of cold water for him. The community was always full of life and activity when he visited.

Truth be told he enjoyed working in the Ontario wilds; of course, he could do without the annoying insects that were out for blood.

Monday morning, bright and early, before he had had his first eye-opener of the day, he sat in an uncomfortably hard chair in his supervisor's office waiting for her to arrive. The room was cold and the pong of stale cigarette smoke hung in the air and an ashtray filled to overflowing with menthol cigarette butts was perched precariously on the edge of the desk. Laura Deboom was a career-oriented company woman and she was late. Nick wondered if this was a ploy to make him impatient hoping he would leave. He was patient but he was meeting with his Association Rep, Enzo Watt in forty-five minutes.

Twenty minutes later and just as he was about to leave she arrived in a whirlwind enveloped in a cloud of tobacco stench trying to let on she had been otherwise engaged with something more important than him. She had barely sat down when she took out a cigarette and lit up without so much as a by your leave.

He watched her eyes glaze over as he explained the risks of one-man line crews, which she was well aware of, and that he considered his deployment unsafe. She made it clear to him that he was wasting his breath, "I'm sorry." She said disingenuously. "My budget has been cut and there's no money in the budget to deploy two men to a job. It's out of my hands."

He left the meeting frustrated and infuriated that she, and by extension, the company, put profits ahead of their employees' safety.

Ten minutes later he was seated in the local coffee shop, across the table from the Association Rep., Enzo Watt, each with a large, steaming hot double, double on the table in front of them. "Where have they got you working, Nick?" asked Enzo, trying to get the conversation started.

"Laura Deboom has got me running a line into Thelost Village, north of Allegory Park, *alone*. That's what I wanted to talk to you about. We've had Association meetings on the hazardous practice of one-man line crews and we've seen firsthand what can happen in those circumstances.

I've just come from a meeting with my supervisor, Laura Deboom, and she refuses to arrange for someone as a second remote deployment. She says it's out of her hands due to budget constraints."

"Money's tight that's for sure. They're redecorating the executive offices you know." Enzo replied seriously.

"Ya well I want to put in a grievance, Enzo."

"Well, Nick, it's a long process you know. And as old granddad used to say, "It's not fair that people are seated first-come, first served. It should be based on who's hungriest." There are forms to be filled out and evidence to be gathered. I'll have to inspect the work site and check for available linemen. Not to mention get in touch with the head office accounting to assess the budget as well as obtain all correspondence that pertains to your deployment.

Even after all of that, it could still end up in arbitration. But if you still want to go ahead with the grievance stop into my office before you go back and I'll give you the necessary forms you'll need to complete, sign and get them back to me next time you're in town." Watt said disinterestedly in an irritating monotone.

Nick was determined to see this through so he followed Enzo to his office and was taken aback by the plethora of forms required. "I had my patience tested. It's negative." He said to Enzo and decided he would have to take them back with him after all and complete them in his off time but now he needed to get back to work.

He went home to gather his things. It was getting on for lunchtime so he made himself a couple of cold roast pork sandwiches and washed them down with a soft drink. After lunch, he packed up his guitar which helped him pass the lonely evenings, and placed it carefully into the trunk of his Camero then climbed in behind the steering wheel and set out for The Last Resort.

A cold drizzle made the roads slick and played havoc with visibility. There wasn't enough rain to run the wipers, even on low intermittent, and too much rain not to keep flipping the wipers on periodically. A few wet snowflakes landed on the windshield and melted immediately upon contact with the warm glass. Nick thought to himself, "What a thoroughly depressing day. Well, at least this weather will give me time in the hotel to fill out all this paperwork."

The drizzle had been replaced by a Scotch mist. His headlights reflected off of the impenetrable swirling wall of white. He switched to low beams and slowed down to a virtual crawl.

He fought to stay vigilant for any wildlife that could suddenly dart out on the road. Struggling with mental fatigue his eyelids felt like lead. It was at that moment that a flash of movement at the furthest edge of his peripheral vision caught his attention. Glancing over his left shoulder he thought he saw something shadowy keeping pace with him. The diffused light of a ghostly moon just rising above the treetops produced an enormous, indistinct silhouette of something monstrous that blended into the trees behind and disappeared.

The remedy for fear of the unknown is to become acquainted with that which you fear.

Alert now, the fog of fatigue was gone as beads of cold sweat trickled down his back. *What had he seen? Was it just his melancholy, weariness and imagination working overtime? He could sure use a strong cup of coffee.* The one thing that was clear in his mind, he'd be glad to get to The Last Resort.

A low growling could be heard emanating from his stomach as it let him know it needed sustenance. It was Monday evening and The Last Resort's Only Hope Restaurant's chef, Howard M. Burgers, would be serving last week's pickerel, microwaved in butter, refried beans refried and leftover mashed potatoes with black currant pie for dessert.

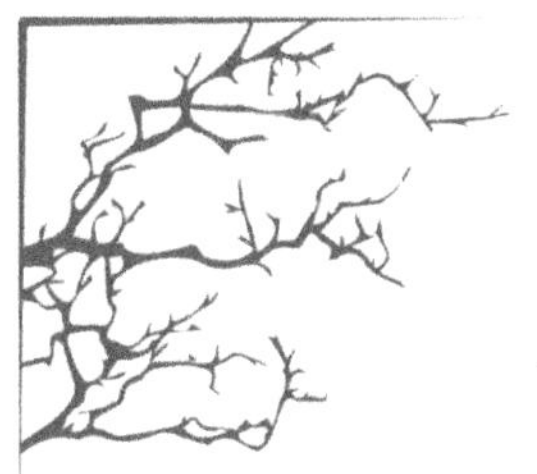

4 Nick's Brigadoon

After an evening spent filling out forms and a restless night of nightmares involving hideous creatures turning his line truck over with him in it and then attacking the villagers, he awoke exhausted and covered in perspiration.

A bright new day full of promise greeted him; as he threw open the curtains. He turned on the radio and checked the weather forecast. The high for the day was to be 20° Celsius with an easterly breeze of about 18 to 20 kilometres per hour, perfect for working in the bush. He washed, dressed and went to the Only Hope Restaurant to pick up his morning double, double climbed into his rubber-tracked utility vehicle or UTV and set out for the job site.

Twenty minutes later he arrived at his work site and pulled up beside the digger derrick. Nick had his mouth set for a couple of delicious biscuits left for him every morning. He found it somehow comforting to know that someone appreciated what he was doing. Opening the truck cab door he looked on the seat, the usual location, but was let down when he found the cab bare. He searched his truck thoroughly and came up empty-handed. "That was both disappointing and disconcertingly odd." He thought to himself. "Well, I'll just have to take an early lunch." He said under his breath.

The morning wore on and no one brought him a cold drink of water. Something didn't seem right. It wasn't like them. "I'll take a ride up to the village when I finish for the day." Absorbed in his labours eleven thirty rolled around quickly. After setting the next pole in place he climbed into the utility vehicle and headed back to The Last Resort and the Only Hope Restaurant for lunch.

He ordered a Road Kill burger and fries and washed it all down with a large Muddy Water (chocolate) milkshake. Then he had the waitress fill his water bottle with ice water and left. All the way, back to his truck he had the uneasy feeling something was wrong in the village. He made up his mind that he would pay them a visit after work.

Within three feet the auger hit a boulder which had to be removed or drill a new hole. The engineer had marked this spot for the pole so he decided to pull the auger up and remove the obstacle. He climbed into the mini excavator and after about an hour and a half his efforts were rewarded. He rolled the one-and-a-half-ton boulder into the bushes and set to work preparing the hole for the pole. By four o'clock he had the pole in and set. It was time to pay the village, a visit so he mounted the utility vehicle and set out to check on the village.

Within twenty minutes he reached the outskirts of the village of Thelost nestled along the shores of Gonemissing Lake. He could see the silhouettes of the tiny cabins as the sun began to set behind them but saw no people bustling to and fro, no sounds of children playing and there were no barking dogs greeting him. Shutting off the motor of the UTV he listened, there wasn't a sound, not even the birds in the forest or frogs in the swamp. There was an eerie hush as if nature was holding its breath, waiting. But what was it waiting for? He also noted that not a single chimney had smoke rising from it. The expected sounds of laughter and conversation from within the cabins were replaced with a deathly silence.

He went first to, Zeke Himphurst, the elder's cabin and knocked on the door. There was no response so he knocked harder and again there was an eerie stillness within. He tried the handle and found it unlocked. Opening it a crack he peered into the dim light filtering through tiny windows and called loudly, "Mr. Himphurst, are you home?" and his only reply, was a deafening silence. Opening the door further the room appeared untouched. The table was set for an evening meal for one and a pot sat on the stove. Nick did not enter for fear of intruding.

Next, he tried the chapel but finding it empty went next door to the schoolhouse. Also vacant, a Cooey .22 stood leaning against the wall by the door. Nick sniffed the barrel for the smell of gunshot residue and checked the chamber for residue. It had been recently fired. A message both cryptic and chilling was written on the chalkboard, "They have come. What do they want? No escape."

Unnerved he began anxiously but methodically checking out all the cabins hoping to find telltale signs of mass exodus. He discovered that all of the cabins were stocked with the kinds of foodstuff and weapons that never would have been abandoned by their owners. In one cabin he found a pot of stewed venison still warm on the table set for a family's dinner. In another a pot of charred stew that had bafflingly been left on the stove and a child's half-mended coat draped over the back of a chair, the needle still embedded in a stitch as if someone had abandoned their effort mid-stitch.

Nowhere were there signs of a struggle or turmoil and Nick knew that no matter what the circumstances that to spontaneously desert their community without their weapons, tools, food and clothing would be utterly unthinkable.

Before leaving he scanned the perimeter of the village in the hopes of ascertaining what direction the villagers had travelled in, but could not find the slightest trace of their departure no matter how hard he searched. They had disappeared as if they had been apparitions in a dream vanishing at the first rays of daylight.

Adrenalin pumping through his system and beads of the cold sweat of fear on his forehead and running down his back he clambered aboard his UTV setting out, with all the speed the machine could offer, for The Last Resort to call the police.

It was seven o'clock when the two officers finally arrived at the hotel, introducing themselves as Lt. Rob Banks and Sgt. I. Slack. By that time a very agitated Nick had had time to calm down. After relating the bizarre tale to the authorities he was told, "You'll need to come with us, Mr. Tchotchke." The two officers and Nick climbed aboard the UTV and headed back through the bush to Thelost Village. The light was fading quickly and clouds of ravenous insects were out for blood as they drove. It was dusk when they arrived brandishing flashlights and calling out as they quickly made a cursory search. Just as the officers made the decision, to call off the investigation for the night Sgt. Slack stumbled, almost literally, upon the village cemetery. In the fading light, he had almost tumbled headlong into the pitch-black yawning maw of an open grave. It was empty.

Hearing his terrified calls for help Nick and Lt. Banks sprinted to the sound of his voice. "Where are you, Sergeant? Stop messing with us." called a perplexed and distressed Banks.

"I'm down here, sir!" Shouted the hapless Slack.

Both men suddenly became aware they were in a graveyard. Nick cast his light about until he saw the fresh mound of earth beside the darkened void he was just about to step into. "Over here." He yelled to Banks who came running.

"Are you hurt, Sergeant?" Banks called down to his subordinate.

"Just shaken up, sir."

"Give us your hands, Sergeant." The lieutenant ordered.

"Yes, sir." He replied, reaching up.

They pulled a panic-stricken Sgt. Slack, trembling and covered in dirt from the abyss.

The three men were manifestly frightened but tried to put on brave fronts, each not wanting their companions to know how truly terrified they were as they returned to the waiting UTV. Their senses on high alert they quickly clambered boarded the machine that bounced, lurched and careened along the very rough terrain of the trail through the darkened bush towards a modicum of civilization. The weak yellow beam of the vehicle's single headlight cast creepy shadows. Several times Nick thought he caught something dark moving silently through the underbrush to their left, keeping pace with them.

Upon their return to the hotel Lt. Banks advised, "I suggest you try to get some rest, Mr. Tchotchke. We'll be back at first light with a team to conduct a thorough search of the area. Good night."

It was the crack of dawn the next morning that found Nick shivering in the cold and damp as he sat in the cab of his UTV with a steaming cup of Joe in his hands ready and waiting for the police search and rescue or S & R team to turn up. He didn't have to wait long before the first of the trucks arrived with all-terrain vehicles or ATVs on trailers.

Coffee and donuts were being provided by the Only Hope Restaurant and served by Chef Howard M. Burgers, personally.

Everyone had arrived, offloaded their ATVs, geared up and with eye-openers in hand awaited their orders from Lt. Banks, the S & R team leader. Next, police-issued two-way handheld radios were distributed and the Lieutenant directed his officers to secure any weapons found in their search. Finally, after admonishing all the two-man teams on safety procedures they set off.

Entering the lifeless village they were witness to a macabre scene. Behind each of the cabins were chicken coops where every last bird lay dead. This gruesome discovery prompted Nick to investigate the barn at the furthermost edge of the village and the pasture beyond. As he approached he saw what he dreaded, the bodies of several goats and sheep lay in clusters about the barnyard. He parked his UTV, the stench of death assaulting his sense of smell, and entered the barn. Inside he found the corpses of two milk cows and five others, eyes rolling and displaying obvious signs of distress.

He immediately radioed the lieutenant to report the gruesome incidents and as he stood looking out the barn window he noticed several beef cows all in a circle facing out in a protective posture, some staggering.

Straight away the lieutenant hailed the entire search team ordering them to evacuate the village.

Nick's radio crackled as he heard the frantic voices of two members of the search party calling Lt. Banks for help. They were calling from a potato field about half a mile down the lane from the barn. Jumping into his UTV Nick sped off up the lane. He didn't get far before he heard the wild squeals of terrified horses.

Reaching the field the scene he witnessed was one of violent chaos. Two enormous draught horses pulling a plough had become tangled and were in a furious panic. Squealing and thunderous snorting filled the air as the terrified beasts thrashed, their eyes wild and nostrils flaring. It would be difficult if not impossible to get near them let alone to calm them but Nick knew he had to try.

Stopping his UTV he leaped over the fence just in time to see one of the horses collapse from exhaustion and fright. The whirling hooves of the other feverishly flailing horse were relentlessly pummeling its partner. "Watch out!" yelled the three members of the search party as they looked on, frozen with dread.

He was aware of the imminent and life-threatening danger the flying hooves presented but it was now or never. Approaching from the rear of the plough he inched forward until he could take hold of the rein and held it firmly as he spoke soothingly to the normally gentle giant. He must remain calm because horses can sense your fear so calming himself he took out his lineman skinning knife and cut all of the harness that held the thrashing animal captive.

Once the animal was free he released his grip on the rein and allowed it to escape. It wouldn't go far in the fenced field.

He knelt beside the prone horse with gaping wounds on its flank and ribs from the flailing hooves listening and watching for any signs of life but sadly the animal was gone. At least he had saved one of the terrified beasts.

He would let the other one calm down before approaching. Where had the farmer gone and why would he not have unharnessed the horses before leaving the field?

"Wow! That was amazing!" The three relieved onlookers said in unison shaking his hand until Nick thought it would fall off.

"Go see if you can find a bale of hay and maybe a few apples and bring them back here. I'll stay here to watch our upset friend," replied Nick.

A bale of hay and a few apples were found and brought back and the pair opened the bale and threw the hay and apples over the fence while the gentle giant kept a wary eye on them from a safe distance. Nick hoped he would make his way cautiously over to the food when he felt it was safe.

Back in the heart of the village Sgt. Slack was observed aimlessly wandering in circles and muttering incoherently to himself. Lt. Banks was also struggling to maintain lucidity. His mouth seemed unusually dry, he was finding it difficult to focus, and he was sweating.

Nick's radio crackled again. It was Lt. Banks, his speech slurred, sternly demanding to know where they were and ordering them to halt the search for the day. He didn't want to risk the potential infection of any of the searchers with whatever was killing the animals and sunset was fast approaching. The search party gathered in front of the school house where the lieutenant thanked everyone for their hard work and directed them all to assemble back at the hotel for debriefing.

The rest of the evening was spent speaking with the police and writing reports. Lt. Banks had assured Nick that they would be heading back out to the village to resume their search in the morning without civilian volunteers. The hotel was now under quarantine until everyone had been checked over by the Hazmat Team for possible biological or chemical contamination. He had made arrangements for a Hazmat Team including a physician to join them as soon as possible. He had next contacted the Forensics Team and a team of Veterinarians to get to the hotel for briefing first thing in the morning.

The lieutenant, clearly more than a little worried about his Sergeant and their situation, was beginning to feel more like his old self. The physician called in, Dr. I. C. Graves, insisted that he check him over, against Banks' protestations, and determined he was fit to resume the operation.

The doctor gave Sgt. Slack a thorough examination and determined he too was fit and ready for duty.

The news media had gotten wind of the unfolding mystery of the vanishing village and the first of their ilk was being held off a few miles from the hotel by a police roadblock. Lieutenant Banks had issued a statement, "It is too early in the investigation to come to any conclusions."

The next irritant to arrive was the tinfoil hat brigade. Their harebrained theories and conjecture included UFOs, wormholes and mythical beasts.

The debriefing was finally over at about ten p.m. Nick entered the packed restaurant to have something to eat and then was off to bed. He knew his sleep would be haunted by visions of the look of abject terror on the face of the Suffolk Sorel he had freed from certain death that afternoon. A normally easy-going Goliath of the farm, standing 16 to 17 hands or 65 to 70 inches tall, weighing about a ton and possessing an indomitable spirit.

5 Gogh is Going, Going, Gone

Nick awoke at first light to a hubbub of car doors opening and closing, loud voices, shouted orders and equipment being unloaded and loaded outside. The whumpa-whumpa-whumpa sound of a helicopter rotor could be heard hovering overhead. Looking out his window he saw a crowd of men and women all preparing to make their way to the ill-fated village. It looked like a scene from a science fiction movie. He recognized some of them as scientists from the Hazmat team that had kept everyone up half the night prodding, poking and taking bodily fluid samples. The others milling around must be Forensics and Veterinarians.

The Hazmat team had given everyone a clean bill of health. Lt. Banks had given the official okey-dokey for all of the civilian participants to return to their normal; everyday lives if that were possible after what they had witnessed.

Nick was still worried about the terrified Suffolk Sorel so he left his room and buttonholed one of the Veterinarians. After explaining his concern they exchanged contact details with a commitment to talk again in a couple of days.

Nick spent the morning hooking up the flatbed trailer to the truck, loading the UTV, mini-excavator and his Camero onto the trailer and making sure he hadn't left any tools or personal items. It was now lunchtime so he ordered a sandwich, a slice of apple pie and a cup of coffee before climbing into the cab of the truck and setting off for home. He thought about the horse and hoped it had calmed down enough to eat something. Then he thought of the shy young woman that had kindly brought him cold water when he was hot and thirsty and the biscuits and eggs for breakfast. He prayed she and the others were alive and well where ever they were. "I wonder if I'll ever see her again."

His sleep had been haunted by dreams of the sorrel and the face of the beautiful young woman.

He spent the next day cleaning and organizing his tools, washing the truck, utility vehicle and excavator, and checking the truck's tires, lights and fluids in preparation for his next assignment.

He was just finishing up when Line Foreperson, Laura Deboom, strode purposefully into the truck bay with a sheaf of papers in her hand. Stepping right up to Nick and placing a hand gently on his arm she said in her husky voice, "Well, I understand you're a hero. Will you let me take you for a drink after work so you can tell me all about it?" The heavy stench of cigarettes made him take a step back.

"I'm busy after work." Was all he said without looking up from his labours.

Taken aback, she replied icily, "I've got a line repair job for you over in the county. Step into my office and I'll go over the details with you."

The next morning he was on his way to Prince Edward County to replace two poles and repair a line. Later that day, tired and hungry, he returned to his hotel, showered and dressed but feeling strangely anxious he thought of calling the Veterinarian. Picking up the phone in his room he got an outside line and dialled the doctor's number only to get his answering service so he left the hotel phone number and asked the doctor to call him.

After polishing off a hot hamburger sandwich with fries and gravy he paid his bill and went for a walk. Upon his return, he went into the pub to watch television but he couldn't shake his unease and just as he was about to leave I walked in accompanied by Nack, Hugo, Moose and Lawson.

He greeted us with a wide smile and enthusiastic, "Well, I'm sure glad to see you guys."

"We just happened to be in the neighbourhood." I offered but either no one heard or I was summarily ignored as usual.

"We heard you had a little excitement up north." Said Lawson.

"Ya, what was that all about?" asked Hugo.

Nick became very serious, responding, "Ya, I don't know what happened to the village. I still can't believe it."

"Is there a Nick Tchotchke, here?" The man behind the bar called out. "Call for, Nick Tchotchke."

Nick stood up and went to the bar to take the call. He returned to the table with a smile of relief. "Well, at last, some good news. The horse I rescued from the plough is going to be okay." He told us about his wild rescue of the entangled plough horse.

"Wow!" I said as we all listened to the terrifying ordeal.

"Still no word on what happened to the villagers?" asked Lawson.

"Nope; it's like they vanished into thin air leaving their most essential belongings behind and abandoning their animals." He replied, then looked at his brother and asked, "Hey Nack, what is scopolamine?"

"Why? Do you get car sick?" asked Nack.

"The vet said he found traces in the horse's blood."

"Really? It is in the class of drugs called anticholinergics that block the neurotransmitter acetylcholine. It's very dangerous. I wonder how the horse got into it. Did you see any woody shrubs with long thin oval-shaped leaves and long, narrow, trumpet-shaped flowers?" asked Nack, clearly perplexed.

"No. I didn't see anything like that."

"I wonder how the horses would have come in contact with the plant?" wondered Nack out loud to himself.

"Sounds like an X-File," Moose said, adjusting his glasses. "There have been many documented cases of mysterious disappearances and inexplicable vanishings of individuals and whole communities throughout history.

This sounds like the bizarre legend of the vanishing Village of Angikuni; a community of about thirty men, women and children that vanished without a trace in 1930 in Nunavut. To this day no one has any idea what happened."

But Nick hadn't heard him for his mind was somewhere else. Big smoky-blue eyes looked out from an angelic face framed in silky, golden tresses was all he saw. He could still hear her voice so soft and cool, as her scent seemed to drift on the breeze of his reverie. He was Twitterpated.

Wendigos Walk Among Us

The third of three adventures in the trilogy of Chasing the Wendigo as told by

Justin Case

1 That's What Friends are for

Two are better than one, because they have a good return for their labour. If either of them falls down, one can help the other up. But pity anyone who falls and has no one to help them up. Also, if two lie down together, they will warm. But how can one keep warm alone? Though one may be overpowered, two can defend themselves. A cord of three strands is not quickly broken. - **Ecclesiastes 4:9-12 NIV**

Anticipation mounted as I waited with my knapsack packed and wearing my new Peril hiking shoes. I looked forward, with mixed feelings of eagerness and angst, to the annual May 24th fishing trip into the interior of Allegory Park with the guys. Scrambling over slippery moss-covered rocks, roots, fallen trees and numerous other obstacles while carrying canoes and sixty-pound packs on our backs was always a challenge and each year I hoped I wouldn't let Nick, my canoe partner, down. They say, what doesn't kill you gives you a set of unhealthy coping mechanisms and a dark sense of humour.

My five school chums, twins Nack a chemical technologist turned tin can installer, Nick a string erector, Lawson a tin can installer, Hugo a pilot (he piles it here and he piles it there) with the railroad, and I, a Termination Agent for the Tin Can Communications Company, had encountered life and shared adventures since grade seven. Billy, one of Bonnechance City's finest, was a recent addition to the group. After graduating high school we kept in touch with poker nights and weekend getaways to the summer party town of Alexandria Bay.

Nack, who was teased now and then by Nick for his fussy and sometimes squeamish tendencies, meticulously made all the arrangements with Allegory Provincial Park for the camping trip and rented canoes from Allegory Outfitters each year. We had our final meeting to discuss the necessary provisions for the weekend. Lawson and I had gone shopping on Wednesday to purchase the food items on our list which concluded our preparation.

It was the twenty-fourth of May weekend, the opening weekend for Ontario's provincial parks. Morning dew glistened on the grass and shrubs in the cool dampness of first light. The golden rays of the early morning sun were expunging the last vestiges of the night's shadows when I heard the honk of a car horn. Grabbing up my pack I hurried out the door to see Nick Tchotchke pulling into the driveway with Lawson D. Woods riding shotgun. I found a spot in the trunk for my gear and we left to rendezvous with the others at Nack's place. We would divide the groceries as evenly as possible when we reached the access point.

At last, we were on our way and after a brief stop at Nack's to meet up with Billy Aiken, Hugo First and Nack Tchotchke we set out for our next stop, a roadside restaurant for Nack's favourite runny butter tarts. Then we were back on the road to Loose Moose to pick up requisite supplies from the Brown Pop Store and Hooch Control Board before our last stop, Allegory Outfitters, then offloading at Gravel Lake.

Leaving Loose Moose we continued our drive to pick up our rented canoes from the Outfitters and then on to the Gravel Lake access point where we unloaded the cars, divided the supplies, and loaded the packs and canoes. It was then that it became abundantly clear that Hugo packed light. Each of the weekend cour de bois had a canvas backpack to which we each added our share of the supplies except Hugo. He reached into the trunk of Nack's car and lifted out a large plastic garbage bag and began to pack his share of the supplies into the garbage bag. That, we realized *was* his haversack containing his camping gear, a frying pan and more large plastic garbage bags. We would find out as the weekend progressed that the bags, it seems had a myriad of uses from rain gear to a ground sheet.

I raised my Brownie Starmite II and snapped a couple of shots of the guys before loading the canoes and setting out on our great adventure.

Hugo and Nack climbed into Nack's canoe, Nack was the only member of the group that owned his canoe, Billy and Lawson were next to shove off from the landing with Nick and me close behind. After we negotiated the shallow water, weeds and branches in the small stream we entered Gravel Lake.

The tag ends of the real world slowly slipped away as we dipped our paddles into the dazzling water in peaceful synchronicity, gliding smoothly over the surface of Gravel Lake with tiny wavelets lapping against the canoe sides. We watched as a denizen from the depths of the lake breached the water's surface stirring the primal instinct of the hunter in the band of weekend warriors.

Arriving at the farthest tip of the Lake we disembarked and made ready for our first portage. The air was cool, the sun bright and the trail dry, all indications that this should be a pleasant portage. That is until Hugo spotted my new hiking shoes. "New shoes, Justin?" he said with a mischievous smirk.

Hugo took great delight in baiting and torturing me. I guess I was an easy target because I rose to the bait every time.

"Yup," I replied with pride and trepidation. I knew Hugo was just waiting for an opportunity to torment me.

"Do you think they'll last?"

"They're Perils," as if that said it all, "nice and light and cool for hiking," I said defensively. Everyone was looking at my shoes now making me wish I had worn boots instead and brought running shoes.

"I hope you brought a pair of boots with you because you're going to need them." Hugo laughed.

Packs slung on our backs and canoes on our shoulders we set off but as we mounted a small rise a rasping, gagging sound could be heard and then silence except for the panicked voice of Hugo, "Nack! What's the matter?" as he wrestled their canoe off their shoulders to the ground and rushed to Nack's assistance just as he was about to pass out.

Nack had chosen two single strapped satchels in which to pack his personal belongings and his share of the provisions, slinging the straps of the satchels over his head to opposing shoulders. The opposing straps had tightened as he walked until they had quite literally become a garrotte, restricting both life-sustaining air and blood flow. Nack had dropped to his knees just as Hugo reached him and after a brief struggle, with Nack now silently turning blue, managed to liberate his canoe partner from the deadly snare. Coughing and spluttering Nack regained his composure but not his voice. "Thanks." He rasped hoarsely to a very concerned Hugo, after all, he couldn't carry the canoe *and* Nack could he. We all looked on in alarm, unable to help and guiltily restless for the suitable moment to resume our journey. None of us wished to appear unsympathetic to Nack's near tragic end but there were only so many hours of daylight.

Hugo, looking concerned said, "That's what partners are for. Are you ok? Do you need to rest for awhile?"

Nack just shook his head and rubbed his throat still barely able to speak. After the pair secured his packs in their canoe he bravely croaked, "Let's go."

The crisis neutralized everyone, especially Nack breathed a sigh of relief, donned their packs, hoisted their canoes and resumed the portage to Paddock Lake. The rest of our journey was uneventful as we continued the slog, stumbling over huge tree roots that seemed set to trip us up and scrambling over trees downed during the winter snows.

I felt the support of one of my shoes giving way as my foot slid sideways on a slippery root. Looking down I realized, to my chagrin, one of the seams in my new Perils was beginning to let go. Afraid of Hugo's sardonic heckling I limped on trying not to overstress the seam or draw attention to my shoe.

Arriving at the launch site of Paddock Lake we set our canoes in the icy water, removed our packs, loaded up and set out. Pointing our canoes into the slight breeze we cut through the waves on a choppy Paddock Lake. Then stumbled and sweated through a gruelling portage to a short paddle across a gently undulating Goodbye Lake arriving at our favourite campsite. Hot and tired but invigorated, everyone got busy setting up tents and gathering firewood for the night.

Lawson occupied himself over the Coleman stove and campfire preparing our first supper of steaks, potatoes and corn on the cob roasted in the open fire. He took a swig from his box of red wine and wisecracked, "I cook with wine; sometimes I even add it to the food."

I chuckled.

After supper, we gathered up the litter left over from our meal burning what we could and placing the remaining rubbish in the centre of a small blue tarp along with our food supply for the weekend. Nick securely tied the corners together leaving a suitable length of rope free. Next Hugo selected a tree a safe distance from our tents; skilfully throwing the rope over a branch he hauled it up until it was about ten feet from the ground. We hoped this would keep both our supplies and ourselves safe from curious, hungry predators.

Every year we wagered on who would catch the first and biggest fish. Hugo being of a competitive nature was anxiously striving to catch the first fish and had been trolling the lakes on our way in and even now was standing on a giant boulder at the point of our campsite casting his line in hopes of landing the inaugural fish.

"There you stand, outfitted with more equipment than a telephone lineman, trying to outwit an organism with a brain no bigger than a breadcrumb, and yet they manage to elude your bait," I said with a chuckle.

To which he smirked and philosophically came back with, "Fishing provides that connection with the whole living world. Many men go fishing all of their lives without knowing that it is not fish, they are after. Besides you can't catch a fish if your line isn't in the water."

"Scholars have long known that fishing eventually turns men into philosophers. Unfortunately, it is almost impossible to buy decent tackle on a philosopher's salary." I said.

Later that evening I gazed up at the endless frozen blackness of space filled with countless shimmering stars presided over by an ancient iridescent moon. Standing in silent contemplation of the limitless universe I experienced the sensation that someone or something was watching. The hairs on the back of my neck were standing on end as I scanned the darkness of the forest. "It was probably just some animal more scared of me than I am of them." I thought as I stretched, yawned and announced, "It's been a long day I'm heading to bed."

Full stomachs from Lawson's hearty feast, fresh air and the day's trek, not to mention a few adult beverages around the campfire made everyone heavy-eyed. The happily crackling fire had dwindled to glowing embers and we all began to feel the chill of the night as it seeped through our clothing.

Weary adventurers all, we each retired to our cozy sleeping bags to sleep, perchance to dream of catching the elusive "big one".

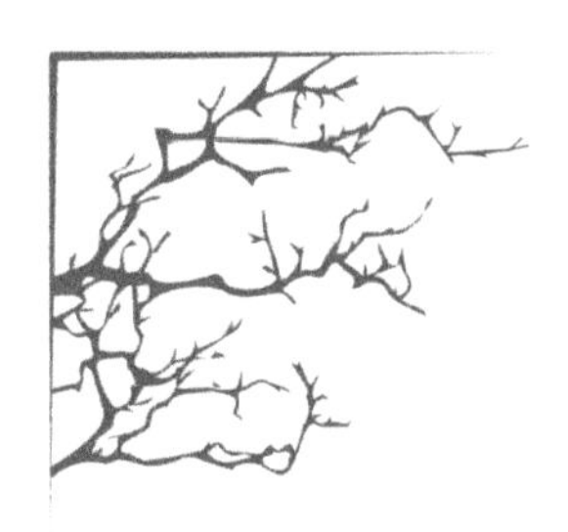

2 Wendigo

Because of the suffering your enemy will inflict on you during the siege, you will eat the fruit of the womb, the flesh of the sons and daughters the Lord your God has given you. – Deuteronomy 28:53

Hugo inhaled the rich toasted almond and cacao aroma of a steaming mug of coffee. He savoured his first sip of the semi-sweet chocolate base tones with black cherry notes and the silky, syrupy feel in his mouth. He watched as the first rays of the sunrise danced and sparkled on the tops of the tiny ripples created by the gentle breeze that agitated the glossy surface of Goodbye Lake. The peace and serenity of early morning in the forest was his favourite time of day. He greeted me by raising his steaming mug in a wordless salutation as I emerged bleary-eyed from my tent, stood up in the frosty dampness of the early morning air, rubbed my eyes, yawned and stretched. "Mornin' Hugo. Ready to catch the big one?"

Hugo grinned, "You bet." He said reaching for his fishing rod.

"Coffee?" offered Lawson who had risen early and seemed to relish the task of cook. After taking care of his morning ablutions, he set to work preparing a hearty breakfast of bacon and greasy eggs.

"You betcha. It smells delicious. Thanks, Lawson." I said accepting the eye-opener with gusto.

Clearing of throats, rustling sounds and incoherent mumbling could be heard as the others slowly shook off the velvety bonds of slumber; drawn by the delicious morning smells and sounds of bacon frying and spitting in the pan, coffee percolating on the stove and toast cooking, soon emerged groggy from their tents. "Mornin'." I said to each one as they emerged.

"Good morning." Called Nack and Billy.

After everyone had helped themselves to an eye-opener of the high-octane go juice and fortified themselves for the day with plates of bacon, eggs and toast we policed our camp and hung out our sleeping bags to air. I remained in my tent trying to, if not repair my shoe, at least prevent it from coming apart any further.

"C'mon Justin," Yelled Nick. "We're leaving."

"Okay, okay. I'm coming." I responded grudgingly as I cautiously pulled on my perilous Peril and hurried to catch up with the others.

Climbing into our canoes we set out on the water to scout the lake for the best fishing spots. We spent the morning circumnavigating the entire lake lingering many times to wet our lines in the hopes there would be a hungry school of trout eagerly waiting for breakfast on our hooks. Alas, there was nary a nibble until...

Scarcely had our campsite come into sight when Lawson said to Billy, "You can't catch a fish without a hook in the water." And with that, he picked up his Pocket Fisherman cocked his arm and swung smoothly timing the release perfectly, for the first time that morning, he watched as the line played out gracefully, then came to a sudden inelegant halt. The line in the Pocket Fisherman had snarled itself into a mare's nest. The bait plopped unceremoniously into the water causing tiny ripples in ever-increasing circles.

Lawson had been involuntarily trolling for what seemed like only seconds when his line went taught and caught off guard he almost lost his gear to the depths of the lake. Dropping his paddle excitedly he attempted to reel in his prize-winning first fish of the trip and vindication that his Pocket Fisherman his buddies had cruelly made fun of was legitimate after all. However, the snarled line of the backlash had locked up his reel tight. "*Quiet, smooth reel action*, they said. *Helps land bigger fish*, they said." Lawson muttered. He was forced to drag his catch back to the beach at our campsite and in exasperation pull the trout to shore hand over hand.

He held up a beautiful two-pound brown trout in obvious triumph.

Billy grumbled, "We fished the whole lake without so much as a nibble and he catches a fish right out front of our campsite."

Hugo shook Lawson's hand proclaiming, "Congratulations, Lawson!"

I slapped Lawson on the back declaring, "Well done you! The first fish, at the rate we're all going might end up winning the biggest too."

Lawson set to work cleaning his fish which he lightly coated in a batter of beer and pancake mix then fried in a pan with bacon grease from breakfast. He enjoyed every last morsel of the delicate fish as we all looked on, our mouths watering enviously, munching our sandwiches.

After lunch, we made our way to the access point to portage from Goodbye Lake to Badger Lake. We wanted to explore our surroundings and try our luck in its deep, emerald-green waters.

I had an uneasy feeling as we hiked along the trail with our backs aching from the weight of the canoes on our shoulders. There were sounds of woodland creatures going about their daily lives all around us in the underbrush. Still, there was something else, an almost indistinguishable sound of something or someone keeping pace and moving stealthily with us. My field of vision was restricted by the canoe to the trail I couldn't get a good look around but I was certain I detected odd cracking and swishing noises of twigs snapping and branches being brushed aside. I even thought I heard a thud as if someone had stumbled but I couldn't be sure that it wasn't one of the guys.

Ever so gently and without warning, my secret fear was slowly becoming a reality. It began with my tongue feeling out of place. Walking on my eyes went askew and finally, my throat separated causing me to stumble. I thought to myself, *I should have worn boots. I must not let on what just happened. I'll just have to tread more lightly.*

If I'm not careful I will lose my right shoe entirely not to mention being forced to endure the merciless ridicule at the callous whim of Hugo. I never quite knew why Hugo baited me. *Was it just for sport? Did he see a weakness he could sadistically exploit or did he actually, think it was funny?*

I had always felt that I was invisible, like part of the furniture. I'm not complaining in fact, I was quite comfortable in my role as a silently analytical observer of human nature.

However, sometimes I was compelled to stick my oar in and I was either summarily ignored or Hugo or Lawson would egg me on and then provoke me. Each time I would think to myself, *Why do I rise to the bait? Never again will I be drawn into another no-win situation. And then, -—I would.*

Upon reaching the lake we set our canoes in the water and stretched out the kinks from the portage. I surveyed the forest and the shoreline for anything out of place or any sign of life. The surface of the lake was as smooth as glass reflecting the trees and rocks along its shoreline. A blue jay in a tree not far away broke the silence with its harsh, jeering call of warning as it took flight disappearing into the forest. Was it warning other creatures of the forest of our arrival or something else? A pair of mallards floating unperturbed suddenly beat their wings in alarm agitating the quiet lake waters and a bale of painted turtles warming themselves on a log in a nearby patch of cattails slipped quickly and quietly into the protection of the reeds. It had become eerily quiet, only the sigh of the wind in the trees could be heard.

The others had seemed unaware of the abrupt retreat and subsequent unnatural absence of wild life sounds, or were they? I shivered as a chill ran up my spine. I hadn't noticed Lawson's stealthy, uneasy scan of our surroundings.

A merry band of adventurers, we set out on the lake in the hopes of catching the *big one*. After fishing around the small lake and coming up empty-handed Nick and I beached our canoe on the opposite shore to stretch our legs and explore.

Our feet ploughed through a layer of last year's damp mouldering leaves of poplar, birch, aspen and oak trees that littered the forest floor from the previous autumn. Underneath the decaying vegetation, insulated from the heat of the day, lay hidden patches of ice threatening, with every step, to twist an ankle or pull a hamstring. The musty unseen clouds of pungent leaf mould wafted upward into the air as we climbed a small rise.

"What is that awful smell? It smells like rotting flesh." Nick whinged. Holding his nose he looked around he had caught the stench of something rancid and definitely, well past its sell-by date.

"It must be a dead animal and it must be close by. You can hear the flies. They're everywhere. It's this way." I replied as I parted the glistening dew-laden pine branches leading the way through the dense undergrowth. We didn't get far before we came upon the carcass of a black bear. It had been disembowelled and its paws removed. We froze in our tracks at the eerie lamenting cry of a timber wolf in the distance and the nearby sounds of movement that seemed to encircle us, "That sounds close!" whispered Nick nervously. We looked at each other and as though reading each other's mind we both turned simultaneously and made our way hastily back to our canoe. I was sure I heard something or someone unseen in the woods shadowing us as we retraced our footsteps.

Reaching the shore we climbed into our waiting canoe and pushed off. Catching up with the others Nick told them about the awful smell of something rotting we had encountered. Billy asked, "Did you find out what it was?"

Nick and I blurted out in unison, "A black bear." We discreetly omitted that we had been frightened off by the howl of a wolf and cracking twigs.

"Someone had cut it open and removed some organs, cut off its paws and just left the carcass to rot," I said, disgustedly.

Billy piped up, "They probably only took the gallbladder. They're most likely already on their way to China as we speak. Say, did you hear that wolf howl?"

"Yup. We sure did and it sounded close." Said Nick.

We all agreed that we weren't catching anything and that there were too many submerged logs and trees, that continually snagged our hooks and lines. It was time to leave Badger Lake and make the trek back to Goodbye. We paddled into a slight breeze that caused tiny ripples on the surface of the lake. It didn't take us long to reach the entrance to the portage. After stowing our fishing rods and tackle we hoisted the canoes over our heads and positioned them on our shoulders for the hike through the woods. Again, I could hear what I thought were the unmistakeable stealthy sounds of small twigs cracking, leaves rustling and branches swishing as something or someone shadowed us. I whispered to Nick, "Do you hear those sounds?"

"What sounds? I don't hear anything except your puffing and panting," Replied Nick.

I couldn't respond I was deep in thought. I love a mystery and right then I was busy running scenarios with the limited clues I had.

Back in Goodbye, we wet our lines in the hopes the fish would be biting and as luck would have it we began to get a few nibbles. Tight lines, warm breezes, good friends, plenty of bait it doesn't get any better.

Then there was a flurry of excitement as Hugo's rod bent under the weight of his first fish. He had hooked a good-sized rainbow trout. Next Nack's rod tip began to quiver then dip and bob as he too reeled in a nice little pan-size brook trout.

Not long after Billy and Nick pulled in a pair of brook trout. Everyone was thoroughly enjoying themselves, except me. I was still brooding over my recent experience on Badger Lake. I couldn't shake the misgiving that I had been close to uncovering something significant, and potentially gruesome and that perhaps the appropriate authorities should be informed.

We fished for another hour with not so much as a nibble, so with the feeding frenzy apparently, over and our own, stomachs beginning to grumble we turned our canoes toward camp and headed for shore. Looking up Lawson thought he saw something black moving about one of the tents. Pointing with his paddle he called to Nick and me, "Hey! It looks like there's a bear around your tent."

Everyone looked towards camp and sure enough, there appeared to be a large black figure moving about our camp. "I can't make out if it's a bear or a man can you, Nick?"

"Nope, but we'd better get back there before whatever it is does any damage. Did anyone put the food away?" No one replied. We were all bent to the task of propelling our canoes as quickly as possible across the lake against a brisk headwind that had just sprung up. Tiny white caps appeared as our lightweight craft was pushed around by the wind rising and falling with each successive wave that lapped vigorously at the sides of our canoes wetting our faces with icy spray.

Sweating and arms aching from struggling against the wind and waves as we raced to reach the beach in front of our campsite; we hurriedly beached our canoes and ran the last few steps to our respective tents. The contents of each were found in disarray but nothing seemed to be missing leaving everyone assessing what they had just witnessed. "We did see someone or something in the campsite didn't we?" queried Billy in his high-pitched voice.

"I'm sure I seen something. What about you Nack?" agreed Hugo.

"Ya, I seen something too." Confirmed Nack.

"Yup, that's right, Justin." Concurred Nick.

Their use of "seen" instead of "saw" made me cringe. "It couldn't have been a bear," I said as I slipped back into my tent and surreptitiously removed my right shoe. Digging in my pack I found a roll of duct tape. I dried my shoe the best I could with my towel and then applied a strip along the separating throat on the inside and another on the outside of my shoe and hoped for the best.

Hugo had laid his bass on a flat rock and challenged everyone, "Let's see who caught the biggest, except you, Justin. I guess you got skunked." He finished with a smirking chuckle.

"Ya, Ya," I said trying to laugh it off.

Lawson had already busied himself combining pancake mix and bread crumbs in a large plastic food storage bag and beating an egg and water in a pan in preparation for breading their fish no one noticed as a canoe silently slipped up onto the beach beside our canoes and two individuals alighted. "Hello," Said the tallest visitor.

Everyone jumped at the unexpected greeting except Hugo. He had been watching their visitors as they crossed the lake landing on our beach and disembarking. "Hello," Said Hugo.

Heads turned to see two Conservation Officers from the Ontario Ministry of Natural Resources approaching them. "We noticed you were fishing. Any luck?" asked a ginger-haired and freckle-faced young woman dressed in olive drab wearing a Tilley hat. "I'm Officer I. M. Shirley Wright and this is Conservation Officer Luke A. Bird.

Hugo, who thought she was as cute as a bug's ear, smiled and said as he made eye contact, "We caught a few; enough for dinner, anyhow."

"Can we take a look?" she responded, blushing.

"Do you all have your licences," Asked her tall reedy partner with a bad complexion and a man bun, eyeing Hugo suspiciously.

After the officers checked our licences they set to work inspecting our day's catch, weighing, measuring and gutting them to examine stomach contents.

Hugo asked Conservation Officer Bird, "We have a little wager on who caught the biggest fish. Can you give us your official weights and lengths?"

Bird gave him a look as if his data was top secret but then acquiesced and handed Hugo a copy of the measurements. "You were all very fortunate today. You are aware, I'm sure, that the legal minimum length for brook trout is thirty-six centimetres and the minimum length for rainbows is sixty-three point five centimetres?"

Beaming with pride Hugo announced the obvious, that his rainbow trout had won, "Sorry guys but my rainbow measured sixty-four point seven centimetres long while all of the brook trout had measured just a little over the legal limit." And it was clear he was not sorry at all.

I said, "Fish come in three sizes: small, medium, and the one that got away!"

Turning to Officer Wright, Hugo, with his most disarming smile, asked "When did the park open?" making small talk trying to keep her attention on himself. It had been two or three years and several more women since he and Heidi had parted company.

"Allegory Provincial Park was established in 1893 and is the oldest provincial park in Canada," Shirley replied with a smile that said she was interested.

When they seemed to have completed their task I approached the officers, "Uh... em. We went over to Badger Lake earlier today and Nick and I came across a rotting bear carcass that had its paws and gallbladder removed."

"Sounds like poachers. Where was this?" asked Officer Wright.

"Well, almost directly across from the portage there's a little beach. Nick and I landed there to stretch our legs and explore a little. We caught sight of what looked like an old abandoned and very large log and stone building some way in the woods and thought we'd take a look. We didn't get more than what, maybe fifty yards, Nick?" I looked to Nick for corroboration; I'm not very good at estimating distance.

Nick chipped in with, "More like a hundred yards when we saw the bear, I'd say."

"Once we saw the bear and heard the sounds in the woods around us we decided it was time to leave." I finished.

An ephemeral emotion flashed over CO Bird's countenance and was gone before I could discern its implication.

The officers thanked them for the information and were set to depart to find the carcass and any evidence that might lead them to the poachers when I asked, "Who lived in that big old log castle, anyway?"

"Gonnar Keep? The three-story, one-hundred-year-old interlocking red pine log and granite mansion was the home of a local eccentric, Gonnar D. Dayz, a uranium miner. He singlehandedly cut, hauled and hand fitted every log and stone. He didn't use a single nail and it's still just as weather-tight as it was when he built it for his family a century ago." Said CO Bird.

"Is there a uranium mine around here?" I enquired. I had been a rock hound and had a keen interest in rocks and minerals.

"Uranium was discovered around the turn of the century and discovered here in the park about 1918," answered Luke as he eyed Hugo.

"What happened to Gonnar Dayz and his family?" asked Billy letting his natural law enforcement inquisitiveness show. He was, after all, a Bonnechance City plod.

CO Bird looked around conspiratorially, with an evil glint in his eye, then, almost in a whisper said, "The little family lived happily for several years until tragedy struck. Legend has it that his daughter, Ina, vanished one night while chasing the pet dog that had run off. His wife died shortly after of a broken heart."

A faint grey mist had begun to creep out of the woods bringing with it the cold and dampness of the surrounding forest creating an atmosphere of gloom and foreboding as the sun dipped below the tree line casting eerie shadows that seemed to be alive. Everyone moved a little closer leaning in toward Luke to better hear him as he told the ghostly tale.

The CO continued, "He never abandoned his search for the young girl and eventually went mad. It is said his ghost still searches for her and late at night his lantern can be seen as amber or green lights moving through the woods. Some say he's become..." he paused for effect then said in a hushed voice, "a Wendigo." He let that last allegation hang in the air smirking as he pictured the weekend warriors, especially Hugo, huddled quaking in their tents with all their lights blazing tonight and listening intently to every crack of a twig and rustle of a leaf.

"What's a Wendigo?" Nick asked apprehensively.

Luke paused to look edgily over his shoulder at the darkness of the forest as if worried that someone or something might be watching and listening; crouching down he motioned for everyone to move even closer as he almost whispered, "Tales of the Wendigo come from Allegory lore passed down by word of mouth from generation to generation for centuries. The story began with someone wandering off too far into the woods and coming face to face with their worst nightmare. They say it is a cunning and beguiling shape shifter that can make even the most perceptive trust and welcome him around their campfire. It prowls the Canadian forests eternally in search of human flesh to satisfy its insatiable hunger."

"H...how w...would you recognize it?" Persisted Nack uneasily and somewhat sheepishly but no one was looking at him. They were all looking at Luke expectantly.

"The first thing you'll notice is the smell of death and rotting flesh. Then you will notice glowing red eyes sunken into their sockets.

It stalks its prey and can mimic human voices.

The Jesuit Relations of 1661 or the chronicles of the Jesuit missions reported that humans became possessed by the wendigo spirit. The men that had been assigned to arrange a rendezvous of the Nations to the North Sea where they were to await the Jesuits' arrival had met their deaths in a very strange manner. It is said that they had been afflicted with more than a canine hunger making them so ravenous that they attacked and voraciously devoured men, women and children until they were finally slain.

The Allegory people say that during the turn of the twentieth century, a number of their people went mysteriously missing. The strange disappearances were attributed to the beast known as the Wendigo." Rapt silence had fallen over the little group, all but one that is.

Much to Luke's annoyance Hugo, unfazed by his attempt to sow the seeds of fear, nonchalantly stepped a little closer to Officer Wright and as their eyes met he smiled and asked, "Is there some way I, um err, I mean we, can reach you if we have any further information?"

Wright blushed visibly, handing him her card and without saying a word turned and joined Conservation Officer Luke A. Bird in their canoe setting off for Badger Lake to investigate the scene of the alleged poaching incident.

"Come on Officer Wright. It's time we were on our way. We've wasted enough time here today." He said, flashing Hugo a look of contempt.

3 Justin IS No Longer in Perils

That evening, we gathered around the campfire for the final night of our adventure, each of us secretly hoping it was not to be literally, our final night. Twinkling sparks from the campfire rose bobbing and weaving their way skyward as if racing to be first to reach the stars only to have their tiny twinkles snuffed out within seconds as each of their lights was extinguished in the cool, damp night air. I surveyed the woods surrounding our campsite, making sure none of my companions saw me, and listened carefully for the slightest sound out of place but could detect nothing ominous. I watched in the flickering firelight as first one and then another of the men did likewise when they thought no one would notice. We nervously lingered around the campfire knocking back a little Dutch courage delaying as long as possible the inevitable call of nature before turning in for the night. No one was keen to leave the security of their friends and the light of the campfire for the foreboding darkness of the forest beyond. Lawson was the first to make his move. I followed quickly and the rest were all hot on our heels, each in his turn lurching a few feet into the trees and staking out his own, patch while keeping the others in sight. Our end-of-the-day chores were completed without incident we bid each other good night and staggered off to our respective tents

We slept undisturbed after the day's activities; the depth of our slumber intensified by fresh air and liquid courage. No one stirred in their sleeping bags as an eerie scene played itself out only steps away.

The night was alive with a cacophony of countless crickets chaotically chirping, the indecipherable high-pitched chatter of the wood frog, sounding like some unknown alien creature, the bullfrogs' deep bass voices and the low, intense hum of the beating wings of legions of tiny ravenous vampires sounding akin to the drone of high-voltage power lines. Silence fell momentarily as the night was split by the blood-curdling howl of the apex predator, Canis Lupus better known as timber wolves, on the hunt.

A solitary figure stood as if transfixed by the radiance from a cold, opalescent orb perched high on the tree tops like a mystic's crystal globe. The icy sphere's reflection shimmered on the shiny black surface of Goodbye Lake while its brilliance illuminated the rocks and trees along the shoreline barely penetrating the wall of trees by more than two or three trees deep. Ghostly shadows seemed to move eerily as if alive. Even the simple process of breathing took extra effort in the oppressive steaminess rising from the damp, rich earth of the woodland and lush undergrowth.

Beads of sweat stood out on a forehead covered with dull, grey dust while cold droplets fell from sodden dishevelled hair to a bare grimy neck and rounded shoulders. A tiny rivulet of blood trickled from one nostril as one eye engorged with blood until it could no longer be opened. Silver flashes like white-hot sparks from a Canada Day sparkler flickered amid an ethereal greenish glow emanating from head to toe of the otherworldly being.

Soft whispering and shuffling sounds could be heard then suddenly, like the tiny sparks from the campfire, his light was extinguished and darkness fell over the campsite once more.

I'm a light sleeper and thought I heard something moving around outside our tent so I nudged Nick, "Did you hear something? I thought I saw a kind of a glow over by the trees."

Nick could only manage an unintelligible, "Umm uh ya ok hmm." and then immediately fell back to sleep.

I put my glasses on but was forced to wait impatiently while the fog on the lenses evaporated. I slipped soundlessly from the warmth of my cozy sleeping bag and cautiously peeled back the tent flap to sneak a quick look. The chill of the night still lingered as dawn's glow was just beginning to spread over the tree tops. I saw nothing untoward and the call of nature was too strong to resist. I shivered as the coldness from the cloth of my shirt touched the warmth of my flesh. Grudgingly I put first one leg then the other into unpleasantly cold, damp jeans, carefully pulled my Perils on, still uncomfortably damp from the day before, and quietly crawled out of the tent. Once out of the tent I rubbed the sleep from my eyes, stretched and yawned while warily scanning the campsite and its environs for any evidence of anything menacing lurking in the shadows. Seeing nothing I ventured cautiously to the tree line looking for a path of least resistance to enter the forest. Finding a suitable entry point I looked down spotting what appeared to be signs of a scuffle and drag marks in the dirt and leaves.

Venturing tentatively into the forest I noticed a faint, almost imperceptible in the daylight, greenish glow in the shadows beneath the canopy of poplar, jack pine, red pine and silver birch. I knelt to get a better look and on the ground found a sporadic trail of recently disturbed sand and soil that seemed to be glimmering with tiny greenish specks.

The traces of glowing detritus quickly became few and far between periodically causing me to have to hunt around to once again pick up the ever-weakening trail. Preoccupied in my endeavours I had failed to notice just how far I had wandered until abruptly the trees and underbrush gave way to a large clearing occupied by a forlorn tumbled down shack. Its door hung precariously by a single rusty hinge, what window panes remained unbroken was obscured by years of dirt and grime and the rough-hewn board and batten walls leaned drunkenly.

Not too far from the shack sat a tall red brick chimney stack with a square base, about six feet by six feet and a yellow fire brick-lined furnace containing a black iron crucible. Next to the furnace, a small red brick building with a rusty tin roof had been constructed.

Without thinking I found myself cautiously crossing the open ground between me and the hovel and peering into the blackness of the half-open doorway. I stood motionless not knowing what to expect then I became aware of a faint greenish glow that seemed to emanate from somewhere deep within the darkness. Yet how could that be? The tiny shed was only about sixteen feet deep.

Voices approaching broke my concentration. I knew I must get out of there and tell the others what I had found. I hastily retraced my steps back to camp where everyone was milling about anxiously.

"Where have you been?" Nick and Lawson asked in unison.

"Guys, guys, come over here. I found what looks like signs of a struggle and a glowing trail. C'mere and take a look.

I think I might have found the poachers." I was out of breath as the words tumbled out.

"Where have you been?" repeated Lawson.

"We thought the Wendigo got you," said Hugo, chuckling mockingly.

"Look here. I followed this faint trail. It looks like radium." I replied as I scooped up my camera that had been hanging on our tent pole and snapped a photo.

Lawson stepped over to where I stood followed close behind by the others. "Watch out. Be careful where you step so you don't mess up the signs of the struggle." I admonished pointing at the tracks in the wet soil and spreading my arms as if to protect the area.

They all looked where I was directing their attention. "Oh, ya; I see the tracks," confirmed Nick.

"Ya, me too," said Nack.

"We should probably get in touch with the Conservation Officers and leave it up to them. Hugo, have you still got how to get in touch with the Yogis? Give them a call. Oh, ya. I forgot you don't have a phone. Give me the details and I'll see if I can get hold of them." Billy who always carried a walkie talkie instructed.

Hugo hesitated, reluctant to part with the contact details of his potential conquest.

Lawson was already several yards into the woods tracing the glow that was rapidly growing fainter by the minute, from the radioactively charged remnants of the sand and dirt strewn as someone or something departed the campsite. He could be heard mumbling incoherently and clearing his throat as he studied the trail. "C'mon. The glow is fading and they could be getting away. How many were there Justin?" he called over his shoulder already moving rapidly down the now visibly travelled path.

"Now where are they going? We should wait." Whinged Billy.

Lawson was a man of action and never one to back down from a good fight.

"At least two; I didn't see them I just heard them talking," I told him as I hurried to catch up. I had always thought that Lawson and I made an unbeatable team. We were unstoppable at handball in high school with Lawson making the finesse plays and winning shots while I had played a supporting role. "Shouldn't we wait for the authorities?" I suggested huffing and puffing as I struggled to keep up.

There was no response from Lawson as he forged ahead. Arriving at the edge of the clearing he stopped and took cover, crouching in the dense underbrush. The others, not wanting to miss any of the action, could be heard crashing through the undergrowth, their feet thumping loudly along the by-now, well-worn trail. Lawson waved wildly for them to quiet down and take cover.

Lawson whispered over his shoulder to Billy, "Are the Yogies coming?"

"No signal," Billy whispered back. "I'll try to find somewhere I can get a signal. Don't let Lawson do anything until I get back." He said to Nick, Nack and Hugo.

"If you look closely, Lawson, you can just make out a faint greenish glow in the darkness at the back of the shack. I think there's a cave in there." I whispered.

Lawson focused on the shed. "I don't see any movement. I'm going for a closer look." Lawson whispered as he moved stealthily toward the shack with me close on his heels.

Apprehensively, all of our attention focused on the open door and the darkness beyond, we crossed the open ground that lay between the cover of the forest and the rickety little shed. Step by careful step we drew ever closer. Crouching beside the open door, all our senses on high alert, Lawson peered into the gloom within for any sign of life, finding none he cautiously stood up and took a very guarded step into the shadows with me following close behind. Worn and rotting floorboards cracked, creaked and groaned under our weight with each careful step.

The suspense mounting, Hugo, Nack and Nick hunkered down in the undergrowth just outside the perimeter of the open ground. They anxiously waited for an opportunity to present itself, to join their comrades. They watched apprehensively as Lawson and I disappeared into the darkness of the tiny cabin.

"Where are they going? Billy said to wait till he got back. We don't even know if the officers are coming." asked a nervous Nack.

The tension was becoming too great for Nick. He motioned to the others nearby, "Let's go." The others didn't need any coaxing. All three left the safety of the bushes and began warily closing the distance between themselves and the shack.

Upon reaching the side of the hut Hugo stole a quick look around what was left of the porcupine gnawed door jamb. "What do you see? Where are they?" enquired Nack and Nick in unison.

"I can't see them but I can smell them. Somebody used too much aftershave. There's no one in here." Replied Hugo as he stood up and stepped through the doorway.

"That's not cologne. That sweet and distinctly erotic fragrance is the scent of Devil's Trumpets or Datura Stramonium a member of the Solanaceae family. Do **not** touch it, it's extremely poisonous." warned Nack.

"Anybody bring a flashlight?" asked Nick.

"Not me," replied Hugo. Nack just shook his head.

"Do you think they went in there?" said Nack worriedly.

"Well, they're not here are they?" replied his brother.

"I wish we had a flashlight. I'm not going in there without a light. There could be bats hiding in there." Moaned a worried Nack who had had a bad experience with a flittermouse or as he called them flying rats.

"C'mon Nack; there's nothing in the dark that isn't there when the lights are on. Except for..." Hugo paused for effect, "The occasional swarm of bats." He said mockingly.

"Ya, well they carry rabies you know." Whinged Nack.

Nack and Nick not wanting to be left behind were on their feet following close behind Hugo. Taking pity on his sibling Nick suggested, "Someone should stay here to watch out for Billy or anybody else that might be coming back." as he hurriedly crossed the noisily complaining floor. Nack, feeling a little guilty at his sense of relief, stepped back out the door and looked around nervously. Nick and Hugo strained their eyes to peer into the darkness of the tunnel searching for any sign of their friends.

"Shush! Listen!" whispered Hugo curtly.

Faint, dripping sounds, indecipherable whispers and what sounded like distant, furtive footsteps could be heard echoing from the tunnel.

Greenish-yellow dots of light spread randomly over the walls and ceiling like tiny stars twinkling in a night sky had greeted them in the inky darkness of the yawning tunnel mouth but had ended within a few feet. Fortunately, I had thought to bring a flashlight and my headlamp. Lawson was wielding the flashlight like a lightsabre and I was wearing the headlamp. Underfoot the floor was wet and slippery with an inch or two of greasy muck making walking treacherous and when I stretched my hand out to touch the wall to steady myself it was slimy and dripping. Our lights illuminated specks that glowed momentarily after our lights had passed, like millions of tiny eyes opening and then slowly closing.

The air that until now had been only damp, cold and fetid had inexplicably changed. The spelunkers looked at each other at a complete loss. The smell, a sweet and distinctly erotic fragrance that had greeted us in the darkness of the shed and then faded, seemed to emanate from somewhere up ahead. The intoxicating scent grew stronger as we advanced. What we didn't know was that it was the heady scent of death.

Lawson came to an abrupt halt as he encountered a steel wall caked in rust. Running our lights over the surface of the obstruction we discovered a small door. There were barely distinguishable signs that it had been opened recently. Only just visible beneath the dirt and grime of time and pitted with rust hung two ominous signs. A sign mounted above the door commanded the reader to: KEEP OUT in red letters. The other affixed to the door itself was a magenta trefoil on a blue background, the internationally recognized 1946 symbol for radiation. A shiver ran up my spine like an electric current. "What had we stumbled upon?" I wondered.

We listened intently but could hear no sound from within. No glimmers of light could be seen leaking from around the old door.

Lawson stopped his hand on the door handle and looked askance at me and I nodded acknowledgement that I was ready to back him up. He tried to turn the handle, gently at first then he quietly applied greater force and finally he felt it give way. He felt the latch release but unfortunately, it was to no avail. It was then he noticed the heavy-duty padlock securely impeding entry.

We could do no more here so we turned to leave but not before I snapped flash photos of the door and surrounding cave walls and floor. The brilliance of the flash split the darkness momentarily blinding me. Within seconds my sight returned and I stooped to retrieve the spent peanut flash bulbs before jogging to catch up with Lawson. Retracing our steps we emerged, blinking, from the darkness of the tunnel, blinded by the dazzling sunlight of a new day making us squint and shield our eyes.

Hugo greeted us excitedly, "What was in there?" was the question on everyone's mind.

"A dead end. We ran into a steel wall and a locked door. We couldn't get any further and there was nothing else in there so we came out." I explained.

I glimpsed Lawson as he strode resolutely across the clearing and disappeared beyond the tree line.

In the meantime, Nack's curiosity getting the better of him, had gone to the small brick structure to see what was in there. He found the door padlocked so standing on tiptoe he looked through the grimy windows. What he saw took his breath away. What his eyes beheld was like looking through a window into the past. There was a laboratory complete with antique glassware imported from Europe, a 19th-century brass microscope with sub-staged mirrors mounted on a walnut base, a field microscope, and alcohol spirit lamps all from a bygone era. On a bench lay an 1880 Letcher blowpipe to analyze minerals in the field including chemicals and apparatus for grinding the samples, heating them and observing the colours of the flame to identify the metals present. Sitting on an old oak desk sat a set of brass chemical balances, a horizontal circle-reflecting goniometer[3]. Lying on the table next to a mortar and pestle he also observed several, dried-up one to three-inch egg-shaped, Devil's Trumpet seed pods commonly known as thorn apples. He felt they held some significance but what? "They seem important somehow but I can't put my finger on it." He thought as he tried to get a better look at them.

Three walls were lined, from floor to ceiling, with glass-fronted cabinets, one of them filled row upon row with chemicals in glass apothecary jars, each labelled in meticulous copperplate handwriting and the second filled with crystal and mineral specimens. The third was a bookcase filled, to capacity with chemical engineering, archeological, and geological textbooks.

He wished he could get in to inspect the equipment and get a better look at those lethal seed pods.

"Where are you going?" I called out to Lawson's disappearing back.

"I'm going to the log house to look around. They could have gone there. You comin'?" He called over his shoulder as he started down a narrow cart path that seemed to lead in the direction of Gonnar Keep the top of which could just be seen over the tops of the gently swaying trees.

"We don't have time. We've got to break camp and head out today." I whinged.

"I'm going. You comin' or not?" said Lawson, his voice fading away as he rounded the next bend in the path.

"I'm right behind you," I called as I hurried to catch up.

"I'll stay here to wait for Billy," Hugo shouted to Nick and Nack as they ran after Lawson and me.

"What did you see in that old building?" Nick asked Nack.

"A fully equipped antiquated geological laboratory and some very lethal seed pods," Nack replied.

"What are we going to do if they're in there?" I asked, between gulps of air, as I caught up to Lawson.

"I'll let you know when I find out," replied Lawson increasing his speed and disappearing around yet another bend in the track.

The seemingly endless trackway gave the impression it meandered for miles. Just as Nick and Nack were thinking of abandoning the mission and turning around, they almost collided with Lawson and me, as we had pulled up short. We all stood staring at the decaying backwoods stateliness of Gonnar Keep.

The peaked roof, only slightly swayback from years of snow loads and weakened by decay, was covered in beautiful dark green, with hints of yellow, moss. Grasping, clinging tendrils of Kudzu, an invasive vine imported from Eastern Asia, were now blanketing the surrounding trees. The greedy invader was reaching out its five-inch in diameter, dark brown and woody limbs and ten-inch leaves, to claim the forlorn old house. It would soon be covered in stunning purple flowers.

Splinters of kindling lay spread about a splitting log in the dooryard and a small pile of the freshly split firewood was neatly stacked by the front door. Even though no smoke rose from the chimney the pleasant scent of wood smoke still hung in the morning air.

I was the first to break the silence, "Wow! It's huge and spooky." Something glinted on the ground at the base of the stairs. It was a small translucent square pouch. I stealthily approached the front of the building and reaching down picked up the tiny packet with what appeared to be the remains of a fine white powder. After inspecting it I carelessly shoved it in my pocket and promptly forgot about it.

Nick said, "Awesome!" and Nack just shook his head in disbelief.

Lawson had already ascended the stairs and had reached the front door. He took hold of the hand-carved, wooden door handle, black from years of use, and lifted the latch and pushed but it didn't budge. "It's locked. They're not here. We missed 'em." He said disappointedly as he began walking around the porch checking windows but they were latched.

I reached for my Brownie Starmite II and used up the last of the film taking photos of Gonnar Keep, the ground floor interior through the windows and its setting.

Billy and Hugo with Conservation Officer Luke A. Bird and Officer I. M. Shirley Wright hot on their heels burst into the clearing in front of the cabin. Puffing like a steam engine under full steam and looking questioningly from one to another of his companions Billy managed to stammer in his high-pitched voice, "Di...did... I, uh, miss... anything?"

"C'mon let's go. We've got to break camp and get home. We've all got work tomorrow." Lawson grudgingly conceded quickly descending the old well-worn stairs to the dooryard.

"Whoa, hold on there. Will someone fill us in on what's going on and why you got us out here?" demanded Bird.

I told the Officers what I had seen that morning and what we had been doing while Lawson interjected with corrections and missing bits.

"We'll need all of your information before you go in case we need to get hold of you." a self-important Bird commanded officiously.

A beaming Hugo seized this opportunity and promptly drew Officer Wright aside offering her his contact details.

Everyone's information gathered Bird released us.

The smell of the rich dark soil beneath our feet filled our nostrils as the heat of the day drew the moisture from the earth. A slight sense of melancholy descended on our little group as this year's adventure was coming to an end mingled with thoughts of returning to our day-to-day lives creating a subdued mood. We busily broke camp, loaded up the canoes and headed out across the lake to our first portage. The humidity made the treks through the forest weighed down under our burdens very uncomfortable. We were silent as we portaged, each man engrossed in his thoughts, quietly reflecting on the events of the weekend.

Somewhere about midway through the final portage, I blew out both my Perils and struggling valiantly was able to reach the parking lot at Gravel Lake without losing them completely. Amid the slings and arrows of Hugo's cruel and relentless teasing, I threw them in the nearest garbage bin making the rest of the trip home in just my socks.

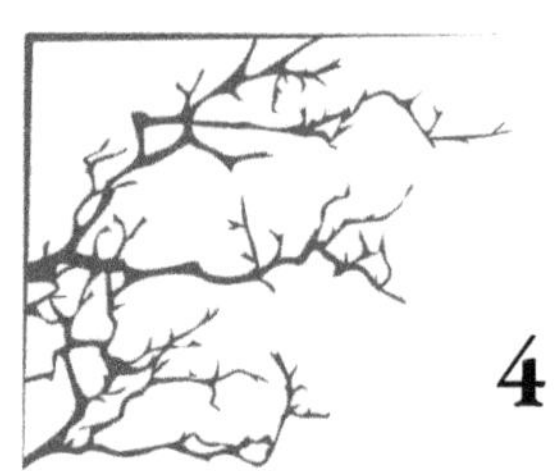

4 Peek-a-boo Zombie

A week had passed since the six intrepid explorers had returned from the bizarre weekend in the wilds of Allegory Provincial Park and we had settled back into our daily lives. However, something very subtle, almost unnoticeable was going on. It was especially difficult; in fact, almost impossible to be absolutely, certain it was happening at all. I was noticing little things out of place. There was nothing I could put my finger on, just trivial things, like cupboard doors and drawers, left slightly ajar and books on the bookshelf out of place. Did I mention my OCD? Did I mention I lived with my parents? Perhaps Mum was just getting forgetful, and yet...

It was Friday evening and I was determined to put my uneasiness out of my mind. I would just relax and enjoy an evening of pool and a late dinner with the guys.

Hugo, always the last to arrive giving the impression he had been torn away from something important, took one look at my shoes and smirked.

I knew what was going through Hugo's mind and it irritated me like the proverbial grain of sand in an oyster's shell.

Nack pondered out loud, the origins of snooker as he chalked up his cue, "I wonder where snooker came from?"

"Oh, why; you're just getting Moose going." I thought.

"Who's going to break?" added Hugo, impatiently, racking up the balls.

"It wasn't created in England but it is British." A string bean of a bespectacled young man who probably tipped the scales at about ninety-eight pounds soaking wet, absurdly yet affectionately, nicknamed Moose, piped up.

Moose curled his lip, sniffed, adjusted his glasses and began, "The origin of snooker dates back to the British army stationed in India in the 1800s. It's a variation of billiards which combined the rules of two pocket billiard games, pyramid and life pool. The pyramid game was played with fifteen red balls and one black positioned in a triangle, while the life pool game involved the potting of designated coloured balls. The rules were formalized by Sir Neville Chamberlain.

The name "snooker" was a slang term for first-year cadets, but Chamberlain often used it to refer to the inept performance of fellow officers at the table.

There's big money to be won in the tournaments." Moose pontificated.

"You don't say, Moose," said Nack absently as he leaned over the table to take his shot. "In the side, off the five-ball." He forecast as he propelled the cue ball with far too much English causing it to carom haphazardly off a red ball before unceremoniously dropping into the corner pocket.

I brought out the photographs I had taken on our Allegory Park adventure and passed them around. There were lots of smiles, chuckles and some good-natured ribbing but something still troubled me about the photos of Gonnar Keep. I just couldn't put my finger on it.

My ruminations were interrupted when Moose pointed at one of the snapshots and asked, pushing his glasses up his nose with a finger, "H...hey Justin. Who's this?"

"What have you found, Moose?" I asked; my curiosity aroused.

Moose handed me one of the photos taken through the window of Gonnar Keep, "You see there, in the mirror?" he said sniffing and leaning over my shoulder pointing to a barely visible face all but hidden by the stairs.

Motes of dust could be seen floating like tiny worlds in the pencil beams of sunlight that penetrated the cabin's gloom. "Ya, it looks like someone hiding behind the stairs. You can only just make out a face. That's what's been bothering me. I couldn't quite figure out what it was. The source of my uneasiness always seemed just beyond my grasp." Relief, like a ray of sunshine glinting off of a brilliant cut diamond, swept over me.

The face appeared wild-eyed with a head of dishevelled hair and a stubble beard. "I'm sure Conservation Officer Luke A. Bird would like to see this. Do you want to give Officer Wright a call, Hugo?" I said with a grin, knowing Hugo would jump at any excuse to call her, as I pocketed the photos and we got back to our game.

"Sure," Hugo replied displaying a brief moment of keenness before the crimson glow of embarrassment crept up his countenance. He stepped outside where he wouldn't be overheard returning minutes later.

Eager to know what would happen next I prodded my friend, "Well?"

"Well, Shirley... I...I mean Officer Wright" he laughed nervously then carried on, "said it was most likely just a trick of the light or a flaw in the lens. She said she would pass our message along to CO Bird and that you should show the picture to the local OPP."

I felt the small polyethylene baggie still in my pocket and made a mental note to make copies of all of the relevant photos to give to the OPP along with a full explanation the next day.

After a couple of hours of playing, sticks and balls, we departed The Break & Run pool hall for the Holin Wah Chinese Restaurant. Moose, being the unofficially designated banker for the group, had collected everyone's share of the table rental. While he went to the counter to pay their bill the others went to their cars, all but one. I was torn between participating in the friendly banter of the group and the feeling that we were deserting Moose, so I hung about to wait for our friend.

I listened as Moose tried to explain to the cashier, who could only speak a few words of English that she had to, 'take their deposit into consideration'. It's funny how we think that if we just speak loudly enough, and slowly enough and enunciate our words clearly, those that don't speak our language will understand. That was exactly what he was doing in a vain attempt to explain our bill to a very bewildered lady behind the counter.

After what seemed an interminable time, Moose curled his lip, sniffed and adjusted his glasses as was his habit, there was a nodding of heads in agreement and smiles as they concluded the transaction.

Moose was still explaining to me what the issue had been as we descended the stairs and exited The Break & Run. Opening the door and stepping into the street we were met by a cloud of moths and other assorted flying nuisances attracted to the light over the door.

Lawson sat, motor running, waiting. "What took you so long?" Moose climbed into the passenger seat of Lawson's car curled his lip, sniffed, adjusted his glasses and began, "Well you know Lawson; I had to get the cashier to recheck her math because she didn't give me the right change. Then ..." They pulled out of the parking lot with Moose still explaining why he was so long.

I had parked my car under the pinkish radiance of a mercury vapour parking lot light close to the pool hall. Approaching my car I got a whiff of the unpleasant pong of cigarette smoke and glimpsed a subtle movement in a remote corner of the lot. A furtive figure shrouded in darkness, appeared to have been waiting and watching.

The phantom figure looked as if it would make its move but quickly retreated as a police car slowly cruised by, the officer surveying the lot for anything out of order.

Not wanting a confrontation I hurriedly got into my car and followed the police car onto the street. I watched my rearview mirror for any indication the mysterious sentry was following but saw nothing. "It had probably just been a panhandler." I thought to myself. The patrol officer and I parted ways at the next stop sign. Arriving at the restaurant I scanned the vicinity for any sign of being observed but found none. "Anyway, the tramp probably didn't even have a car so how could he follow me." I thought to myself.

I spotted Nick's Camero and pulled into the vacant space next to Hugo's Honda Civic I stepped out and entered the restaurant. Catching sight of my friends I could hear Moose holding forth with a dissertation on, of all things, fortune cookies, "It may surprise you to know that fortune cookies are an American gimmick; appearing after World War II for American customers expecting dessert after their meal. After a meal in Hong Kong, you might have red bean soup or an almond cookie."

I made my way to the table and pulled out the remaining chair but before sitting I noticed something on the seat. There sat my Perils, in all their dilapidated glory and smothered in duct tape. I could feel my temperature rise as I went red in the face with embarrassment.

After the laughter and wisecracks faded away I reached into my coat pocket and fished out a green garbage bag. "I was going to offer you a new, heavy-duty, multi-purpose backpack, no expense spared, for our next canoe trip. However, after receiving your very thoughtful gift, Hugo, I'm sure you will understand when I borrow your new penny pincher pack for the evening." And with that, I promptly and unceremoniously scooped the shoes into the garbage bag and placed them beneath my chair.

Everyone had a good laugh and then we turned our attention to the menu. Copious amounts of food were ordered and menus collected I turned to Nack sheepishly enquiring, "Have you noticed little things out of place or missing, or doors and drawers left ajar around your house?" I knew if anyone would notice incongruities it would be fastidious Nack.

"No. No, I can't say that I have, Justin. Why?" my friend replied adjusting his cutlery and checking the utensils for cleanliness.

This drew blank stares from everyone except Hugo who started to smirk until Nick replied reflectively, "Ya, Justin. Now that you mention it I have noticed things were moved but I thought I was imagining things."

"How would you know if something was missing? You're always losing things." Scoffed his brother; gaining nerve from his brother he turned to Justin offering, "Ya, Justin. You know, now that you mention it I have noticed a few things out of place."

At the considerable risk of embarrassment, I plucked up the nerve to forge ahead, "I'm sure someone was waiting in the shadows in the parking lot at the Break & Run. Whoever it was started to walk towards me but a police car cruised by and they moved back into the shadows. I got in my car and came straight here without seeing anyone else suspicious."

Everyone listened politely except Hugo, whose grin broadened as he said, "It must have been the Wendigo. You've heard too many ghost stories about things mysteriously out of place and sometimes disappearing." He chuckled.

"Ya, that must be it." visibly subdued Nick acquiesced.

Nack looked unconvinced but said nothing.

A tense and somewhat uncomfortable silence fell over the group but within a few moments, conversation resumed turning to such hot topics as the next poker game, cars and golf.

Our meal finished we each placed a tip on the table and then lined up to pay our respective bills. After which we made our way to our cars. I nervously scanned the parking lot but could see nothing suspicious. Hugo leaned over and gibed, "Watch out for the Wendigo." Chuckling to himself as he got into his car.

One by one they pulled out onto the street and headed for their homes.

Arriving home I was ticked off to find someone had parked right in the middle of the driveway. I pulled up out front and parked. My irritation growing I got out of my car to confront the trespasser. I recognized Conservation Officer Luke A. Bird standing beside his car with its engine running and illuminated by the house light. "Officer Bird, what can I do for you?" I asked.

Without so much as a by your leave, he said, "Officer Wright told me you had pictures that might help in our investigation?"

Irked I said, "Would you mind moving your car so I can get in my driveway?"

"Sure." He said as he climbed back into his vehicle and backed out.

I got back in my car and drove into the driveway and around the back of the house to park with Bird following. I tried to quietly close my car door hoping not to wake my parents. It was too late. I could hear Tippy barking and scrabbling at the back door to defend her family. She had heard the sound of a strange vehicle entering her domain.

I rushed to get to the backdoor in the hope of settling Tippy as quickly as possible. "I'll get them for you," I said to Bird as I opened the backdoor trying to control and quieten a very protective yet inquisitive dog. Squirming and pulling in an attempt to get to the stranger all the while feverishly wagging her tail and making conflicted sounds of a low, menacing growl and whine of greeting a new friend.

Bird took a step back. "Will she bite?"

"She just wants to be friends," I said as we moved within sniffing range. She sniffed a terrified Bird all over and decided he wasn't a threat.

"You better let me have the baggie as well. I'll pass it along to DSS Oxley Kaye and try to smooth things over for you. They'll make sure the substance gets analyzed."

I went to my bedroom and retrieved the photos and the baggie and handed them to him. "I was going to turn everything over to the police."

"Don't you worry about that; I'll make sure everything is looked after. Where did you find this? Is that all you found?" he challenged.

"I found that single baggie on the ground in front of Gonnar Keep," I said hoping to avoid letting on I had kept what I hoped was enough for Nack to analyze.

"Good night, Mr. Case. I'll be in touch if I have any more questions." He said icily as he turned and left.

"Good night," I said dragging Tippy inside and closing the door.

I switched off the lights and stood in the darkness looking out at the icy blue moon and wondering if I had done the right thing by giving the evidence to Bird. He was not a likeable person but did that make him a suspect? I'll follow up with DSS Kaye tomorrow I thought as I crawled into bed.

5 Last Resort for a Zombie

Hungry, cold and exhausted, his clothes torn and filthy, he stood shivering in the hammering rain his arms hanging limp at his sides. Disoriented he stared blankly at the halo of colours radiating from the rain refracting the glow of a single bug-specked bulb illuminating a sign that read, 'The Last Resort', not knowing what to do. "Should he continue his search or should he go back? What was he searching for? It was so hard to think; to cut through the fog in his brain."

Oblivious to the many frightened eyes watching him from the shelter of the windows of Only Hope Restaurant. Their breath created splotches of steam as they pressed their noses to the cold glass, "Who is he? Where did he come from? Why is he just standing there like that in the pouring rain? Why is he sparkling?" He was covered in pinpricks of light that seemed to ignite in the darkness like tiny sparks from the embers of a campfire and someone whispered, "Wendigo."

After what seemed like forever the owner, Kent Last, yelled for someone to call 911 and grabbing up his coat ran out into the torrential downpour to bring the poor creature into the warmth and security of the Resort.

A murmur of trepidation and incredulity passed amongst the watchers like an ill wind. They stared transfixed as the owner guided the zombie-like figure towards the restaurant door. Once inside the owner took the stranger to his office and ordered a waitress to, "Bring a bowl of Howard's hot soup right away and some towels and blankets."

"You need to get out of those wet clothes." There was no response. Gradually his eyes began to close, "No. No! No, you have to stay awake. Don't go to sleep!" But it was no use; he slowly slumped over onto the sofa. Just then the waitress came in with towels and a blanket. Snatching a towel from her hand he began furiously rubbing him down hoping to wake him, "Start towelling him down. We need to get him dry and stimulate his circulation."

The stranger's eyes still had not opened when the paramedics and police arrived. The paramedics set to work taking vital signs and removing his wet clothing while attempting to raise his core temperature with heat packs. After stabilizing him they readied him for transport to the nearest hospital.

Constable Viola Fuss, who had been temporarily assigned to the Whitney detachment, had been dispatched to the incident and stood watching the paramedics as they worked to stabilize their patient. She asked, "What seems to be the matter with him? Is it an overdose?"

"It appears to be alkaloid toxicity and hypothermia. I don't know which alkaloid yet but I'd say he's been on it for an extended period. The doctors will have a better idea after some tests." explained one of the paramedics.

She delayed their departure momentarily leaning over the comatose form on the gurney to question their patient. "Can you hear me? What is your name? How did this happen?" It was no use. He was out for the count. She had to let them take him. "We'll need a full forensics examination. Bag all his clothes and any contents for evidence. I'll pick them up at the hospital." She directed.

Something was niggling at her subconscious but she couldn't quite grasp the elusive tidbit. "Oh well, it will come to me when it's ready but for now I need to get busy with the basic routine groundwork of establishing the facts while they are fresh." She thought as she turned to the resort owner asking, "My name is Constable Viola Fuss and you are?"

"Kent, Kent Last. I... I'm the proprietor of The Last Resort."

"Mr. Last, can you tell me what happened here?"

"My guests first noticed him just standing out in the parking lot in the pouring rain. When I noticed the commotion I went to the window and when I saw him standing out there I grabbed my coat and brought him in. He was in a bad way, shivering and all at sea I knew we had to get him warm and dry."

"Do you know who he is? Is he a local?" questioned Fuss.

"I've never laid eyes on him before. You might check with my guests or the staff." He replied. "I hope he's alright. May I look after my customers now, please? If I can be of any further help you only need to ask, Constable Fuss." He said starting to rise from his chair.

"That's all for now but I may need to speak with you again." cautioned Fuss.

"Oh, there was one thing, though. Very strange it was. I don't know if you noticed, I don't suppose you would with the lights and all. No, I don't suppose you would especially with the madness, so to speak, and all. It's probably nothing. Maybe it's nothing." muttered the resort owner.

"Go on, sir. What did you notice?" she urged impatiently as she thought, 'In the famous words of Foghorn Leghorn, "Boy, I said boy. You're about to exceed the limitations of my medication."'

"He sparkled." He whispered conspiratorially.

"Sparkled? What do you mean 'sparkled'" she said questioningly.

"He was covered in tiny pinpricks of light that winked and blinked in the darkness like a disco ball. They seemed to emit light, not reflect it as if they were emitting light from within. Very eerie it was too. Ask anyone. They all saw it."

"Yes, alright; thank you. You've been very helpful. Is there somewhere private I can interview your patrons?" She asked, terminating the interview.

"Why, err... yes. You can use my office."

"First, would you please show me where you noticed the victim? I would like to inspect the location you all saw him standing." She said as she rose from her seat.

"Of course, Constable Fuss; right this way. I don't think anyone saw him arrive. He was just, sort of there just appeared from nowhere. We were all shocked, I can tell you. I mean, it's not the sort of thing one sees every day, or expects to see, is it? He was in a sorry state. I'm sorry, I'm babbling again aren't I?" He said, opening the door for her.

Outside Last directed the constable's attention to a spot in the parking lot in front of the sign for The Last Resort. "He stood right here staring transfixed at the light. It was the strangest thing. Even with the rain teaming down he stood there like a zombie with his arms dangling limply at his sides, just staring at the light." He said indicating a place in the gravel where the rain had since washed away the last traces that anything had ever taken place.

Constable Fuss swept the area with her flashlight for any signs at all that might indicate where he had come from such as tire tracks, footprints or anything that might have been dropped but it was no use. After searching the area thoroughly she said, "We might as well go back inside."

"Yes... yes, of course, Constable Fuss. I don't suppose there's any trace of his having been here; oh, what a sad statement." He blathered as his voice began to quiver.

Once seated behind Kent Last's desk she asked him, "Would you please send the patrons in one at a time, Mr. Last?"

Noticing the constable's attempt to stifle a shiver he offered "Anything I can do to help, Constable Fuss? Would you care for a hot cup of coffee?" He turned up the office heater as he turned to leave.

"That would be very welcome. Black, please. Thank you." She acknowledged.

"I'll have someone bring you in a carafe right away. Just let me know if you need anything else. We're only too glad to be of service at The Last Resort." said the resort owner as he backed out of the room.

She questioned each of the six patrons about what they had witnessed and heard virtually the same story six times. Only one had not noticed the sparkles.

The last witness, Ina Dayz, an elderly, white-haired little lady with a toothless grin and a mischievous twinkle in her eye leaned over motioning to Viola to come closer and whispered, "You mark my words, dearie. What we saw was a Wendigo."

A couple, Hugh B. Wright and his wife Eileen had already been questioned, appeared in the doorway, "Are you ready, Mum?" asked the woman.

"We're finished, thank you," said Constable Fuss.

"Come along, Mum," said Eileen putting her arm around the old lady's shoulders to steady her.

Constable Viola Fuss finished her preliminary interviews thanked the owner and left the resort heading for the medical centre. She skillfully navigated her cruiser through driving rain as it hydroplaned along the two-lane highway in the pitch dark. She arrived at the hospital and went directly to the emergency room to retrieve the victim's personal effects and check on his condition.

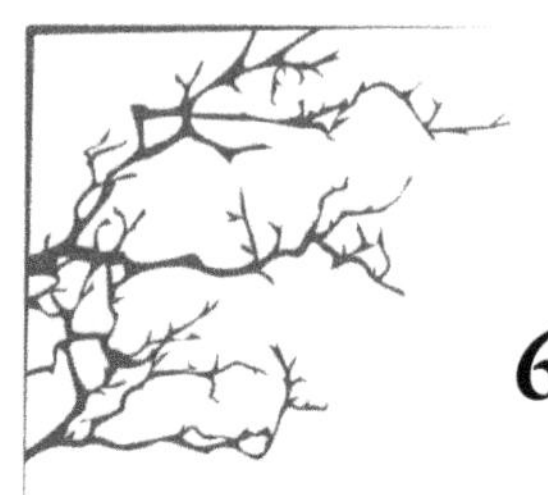

6 A Day at the Beach

I stood in a hallway lined with lockers and a terrazzo floor. I was going to be late for some class I couldn't remember and I couldn't bring to mind which locker was mine. Suddenly I realized I couldn't recall the combination even if I did find the right locker. Walking hurriedly down the corridor and becoming increasingly more anxious as I passed the first classroom door I heard what sounded like whispering.

Like a drowning man rising from the depths, struggling to breach the surface, lungs aching for the next breath, I fought to extricate myself from the clinging, diaphanous tendrils of sleep.

The hot breath on my cheek of someone whispering far too close came again. The fog cleared and I became aware of Tippy gently nudging my arm and panting. "Good morning, Tippy. I guess you need to go out." I said quickly getting out of bed and pulling on some clothes.

Her tail drummed against my closet door in jubilant anticipation.

Mum and Dad were off to work and I guess Tippy was lonely. I tousled her ears and slipped her collar and leash on then left the house for a short walk.

Her morning routine finished I asked her, "Is it time for breakfast?" as we walked up the driveway to the back of the house.

"Okay, just give me a couple of minutes and I'll get breakfast. We're going to visit Heidi and Notcho today with Nick and Nack and the kids." I told her. She cocked her head this way and that as if trying to grasp what I was telling her.

She lay on the floor in the kitchen patiently waiting, her eyes following my every move. As soon as I picked up her dish she scrabbled to her feet, her nails raking the linoleum floor, trying to get her head in the bowl before I had even put food in.

"Wait a minute. Wait a minute." I said trying to keep her from spilling the food before I had a chance to put it down. "There you go," I said.

The ringing of the telephone interrupted my culinary task. My first thought was that either Nick or Nack were calling to cancel but when I picked up the receiver and said, "Hello." I was taken aback when I heard; "Mr. Case?" there was a pause as the caller awaited a response.

"Speaking," I said.

"This is Constable Viola Fuss from the Prince Edward County Constabulary. I have a few questions. Can I come to see you in, say, about ten minutes?"

"Sure, but can you make it about twenty minutes? I'm just getting my breakfast. I'll put the coffee on." I replied.

"Twenty minutes it is, Mr. Case." agreed the constable.

My hankering for pancakes smothered in maple syrup with sausages and several rashers of smoky, crispy bacon on the side would have to wait for another day. I hurried to wash, dress and grab a slice of toast with peanut butter when Tippy got up excitedly from her after-breakfast nap. She looked at me and then ran to the door alerting me to the imminent arrival of a visitor. Just then there was a knock at the door.

I opened the door to Constable Fuss, "Good morning." I said as I struggled to restrain the curious canine sniffing our visitor all over in an attempt to create a mental scent image of the stranger. I stepped aside to allow the constable to come in.

"Oh, hello there!" she said, ruffling the exuberant mutt's fur as Tippy wriggled and grinned foolishly.

"Good morning Constable Fuss. This is Tippy." I said as the dog flopped on the floor and rolled on her back, legs in the air, for a belly rub.

"Hi, Tippy." She greeted. "Good morning, Mr. Case. I won't keep you. I just needed some clarification on something."

"Sure. Let's go in the kitchen." I said.

Tippy danced around vying animatedly for our guest's attention.

"Tippy sit," I commanded offering her a freeze-dried liver treat, her favourite.

I offered the Constable a chair. Once seated at the kitchen table I offered, "Would you like a coffee? I just made it fresh."

"That would be greatly appreciated, thank you; just black, please."

The constable began, "There was an incident at The Last Resort in Allegory Park last night and I'm just following up."

"Oh, what kind of incident? Was anyone hurt? I haven't been to Allegory Park since our canoe trip on May 24th. How may I help?"

"Thank you, Mr. Case, but I'm not here to get your alibi. This is just routine; we're talking to anyone that may have witnessed anything unusual. I understand you witnessed something you felt was suspicious, is that correct?"

"Yes, that's right."

"Can you tell me about what you witnessed?"

"Sure, but it should be in the report I gave to the Conservation Officer."

"I'd like to hear it from you, Mr. Case. You might have remembered something you didn't mention then."

I told her the full story beginning from following the sparkling trail through the woods to the mine and then to Gonnar Keep. I noticed the constable jotting down notes as I did so. Then I told her about the face behind the stairs in the photograph of Gonnar Keep that Moose had noticed.

"I will need to see the picture you are referring to."

"I gave the photo to the Conservation Officer last night. He assured me he would make sure your office received them."

I could see she was taken by surprise but she recovered quickly. "Perhaps they'll come in this morning."

I got up and retrieved the envelope containing the snapshots of our canoe trip and before I could sort out the relevant snapshots she said, "Can I see those, please?" holding out her hand.

I placed the packet in the constable's outstretched hand and watched her face expressionless as she thumbed through the photos and thought to myself, "She'd make a great poker player."

When she had looked at the last snapshot she said, "I'll need to hold on to these, Mr. Case."

"All of them?"

"I'm afraid so."

"Will I get them back?"

"Perhaps; when they are no longer required." She replied vaguely.

"Can I have copies then? At least let me have the negatives."

"I'll see what I can do. I will need the negatives for forensics." She advised.

"What was behind this door?" she asked indicating the photo of the steel door in the back of the mine.

"It was locked but there was a sort of flower scent in the air there."

"I see."

"You never got a good look at anyone in or around the mine or the cabin?"

"I got up early in the morning on our last day and heard what I thought was a commotion in the woods. It sounded like more than one person. I saw something sparkling on the trail and drag marks in the dirt as if someone had been dragged along the trail.

I didn't even know I had gotten a picture of anyone until a friend pointed out the face of someone hiding behind the stairs in Gonnar Keep. That's the photo Conservation Officer Bird took.

When I got back to camp I told the other guys what I had found. They wanted to see if someone needed help, so we followed the trail to the abandoned mining camp in the clearing and the old mine. That's when I took the picture of the big steel door.

The drag marks seemed to carry on up another trail. Lawson thought we should investigate so we followed that trail to Gonnar Keep. That's when I took a picture of the interior and captured the guy hiding under the stairs.

Can you tell me what this is all about?"

"I can't go into detail but I can tell you that this man" with that she slid the photo of an individual across the table for me to look at, "was found dazed and confused outside The Last Resort in Allegory Park last night. Do you recognize him?"

"He looks like the guy hiding in Gonnar Keep.

Could he have taken an overdose of whatever was in the little baggie I found on the ground in front of the cabin?" I was looking at a photo of a rough-looking man, eyes closed, on what appeared to be a gurney. "This photo... Is he dead? Who is he?"

"Yes. He passed away in the night. We don't know the deceased's identity at this time. That's why I'm here, Mr. Case. I hoped you might shed a little light.

What little baggie and where is this baggie now?"

"I haven't the slightest idea who he is. Can't you identify him by his fingerprints or something?

I turned the baggie over to CO Bird with the photo last night. What was in that baggie, anyway?"

"Unfortunately, and this is not for public knowledge, his body has disappeared from the morgue before the autopsy could be completed." Visions of the Wendigo passed quickly through my mind causing the hairs on the back of my neck to stand on end causing me to shiver involuntarily.

"Would you excuse me for a moment while I make a call, Mr. Case?"

Nonplussed I took Tippy into the living room and waited.

"Mr. Case, would you join me please?" she called after completing her call. "The photo and baggie were brought in this morning. The snapshot had slight damage and the technicians thought what you saw might have been a trick of the light and shadow. The negative will be very helpful in ascertaining whether or not there is someone there. Also, the lab couldn't find a trace of anything in the baggie."

"You can see clearly, someone is peering out from behind the stairs. It's not a case of pareidolia." I assured her. "And, I'm no expert but I thought there would have been enough powder or crystals left in the baggie for identification." I thought I witnessed a look of interest flicker across her countenance but it passed so fleetingly I couldn't be entirely certain.

Without missing a beat she said, "Does he look familiar to you?" bringing my attention back to the photo of the dead man.

"Only that he looks like the man hiding behind the stairs."

"You've never seen him before that?"

"No. Sorry." I replied still looking at the photo. My attention was inexplicably riveted to the photo in morbid fascination.

"Well, that'll be all for now, Mr. Case." She declared closing her notebook. "Thank you for your help. Someone will be in touch." She said breaking the spell. Wrapping up Constable Fuss gathered the photos and rising from her chair she turned and walked into the living room where Tippy lay watching us through the doorway. She said, "She's very friendly. Labs are the best dogs." And reaching in her pocket she pulled out a dog biscuit and offered it to Tippy.

There was a slightly awkward moment when she hesitated to take the dog biscuit, but, in the end, the temptation was too great and she gingerly accepted the treat. The Constable took it all in stride never letting on she had noticed Tippy's momentary suspicion.

I said, "Thank you. You have a friend for life now."

"You are very welcome, Tippy. It was nice to meet you and I hope I'll see you again," she replied, stroking her head and with that turned and walked to the door. "Was there anything else you wanted to tell me, Mr. Case?"

"No, I can't think of anything else but I'll certainly give you a call if I do."

Thank you for your help. We may need to speak with you again. I left my card on the table if you think of anything." She said shaking my hand.

I closed the door behind her and after washing the dishes I tidied up. By 10:00 I was ready for an afternoon spent with Heidi and the guys.

Tippy perked up as we were leaving the house and with her head out the window looked around happily at the scenery, her ears flapping and tongue lolling in the wind, as we drove. We arrived at the Heidi's and quickly found everyone waiting for us on the beach.

Tippy and Notcho were excited to see each other, romping and play-fighting. We all had a great time digging holes in the sand, building inuksuks, and walking in the icy water of Lake Ontario. Nack, Nick and I had brought tabletop grills and were busy setting them up and getting the charcoal lit while Heidi, Tippy and Notcho kept their eyes on the kids.

I counted the buns and hotdogs for the third time then I absently reached into my pocket and felt the smooth glass vile containing a sample of the white crystalline powder that had been in the tiny baggie I had turned over to Conservation Officer Luke A. Bird but the contents had mysteriously disappeared. I stood pondering my misgivings about involving Nack when he spoke, "Justin. Hey, Justin."

I looked up startled. "Sorry, Nack; I was lost in thought."

"Ya, I could see that. Do you think the charcoal is ready for cooking?"

My hand hovered over the coals momentarily, "Yup; lots of heat."

Tippy and Notcho came up beside me their noses in the air sniffing the delicious scents of remnants of past barbeques.

Nick asked, "When are we going to eat? I'm starving."

"It won't be long now. We're just putting the hotdogs on."

"Okay."

While I arranged the hotdogs symmetrically on the grills I asked Nack, "Do you still keep your hand in?"

"My hand in?"

"You know. Do you still dabble in chemistry?"

"A little bit. Why?"

"I have a favour to ask you."

"What's that, Justin?" Nack asked somewhat apprehensively.

"You remember at Gonnar Keep I took some pictures and remember Moose pointed out what looked like a guy hiding behind the stairs?"

"Yaaa." He said slowly drawing the word out, his curiosity aroused.

"Well, Conservation Officer Luke A. Bird came and picked up the photos last night along with a small baggie I found at Gonnar Keep. It had some kind of white powdery stuff in it."

"Okay, so the police lab will find out what it is."

"Ya, except the baggie the lab got didn't have any of the substance left in it to test."

"How do you know that?"

"A police officer, Constable Viola Fuss, came to the house this morning. She hadn't seen the photo I had taken at Gonnar Keep of the person behind the stairs even though I had given them to Conservation Officer Luke A. Bird and he had promised to turn them over to the police. She showed me a photo of the body of a man and asked if I recognized him. He was the same man I had caught the picture of hiding behind the stairs in Gonnar Keep.

When I mentioned having turned over the baggie to Bird it was clear she knew nothing about it. She made a call to the station and then she told me that the baggie was empty.

The baggie still had powder in it when I gave it to Bird. How much would the lab need to be able to determine what it was?"

"They'd only need a few grains."

"Well, there were more than a few grains in the baggie when I gave it to Bird. Anyway, I took a sample before I gave him the baggie. It's here in this vile." I said holding out the vile to Nack.

"What! You took some of the evidence?" exclaimed Nack.

"Yup, and I was hoping you would analyze it. However, I'll understand if you don't want to get involved, Nack. I can't be sure of what I'm getting into myself."

"Let's have a look?"

I handed Nack the vile and he rolled it around and looked at the contents thoughtfully. "Leave it with me." Was all he said pocketing the vile.

"Thanks."

"Come and get it," I called. The exercise and fresh air had given us all ravenous appetites. After lunch, we explored the shoreline for sea glass and then headed homeward.

The fun, the sun, the sand, and the fresh air had made us lethargic and it wasn't long before Tippy's eyes were shut and her head slumping. She had fought valiantly against the velvety tides of slumber but had succumbed slipping blissfully beneath the downy waves on the back seat.

I arrived home to find Mum and Dad were out and the door ajar. I warily opened the door and stepped quietly inside. I called out but received no response as I cautiously made my way to the kitchen. Carefully raising the receiver on the wall phone I called the police who instructed me to get out of the house until officers arrived. Ignoring their warning I began to warily investigate. I noticed that all the drawers were pulled out and cupboard doors stood open.

Walking down the hall I entered the living room and was greeted by cushions in disarray, pictures askew and drawers left half open. Someone had been searching for something. I checked the rest of the house and found much the same scene in each of the rooms but could find nothing obvious had been taken.

I had just finished going over the last room when a police car pulled into the driveway. Two officers disembarked, one walked up the walk to the front door the other went to the back. I could hear Tippy barking fiercely from the backseat of the car. One of the officers called out, "Police. Come out slowly with your hands visible."

I put my hands out in front of me and walked slowly to the door. "Is there anyone else in the house?" one of the officers demanded.

"No," I replied.

"Step outside. What are you doing here?" demanded an officious and intimidating officer.

"I... uh, live here."

"Let me see some identification?" directed the officer.

I started to reach for my wallet and both officers recoiled, their hands going instinctively to their weapons. "Slowly; please, sir!" Commanded the one that seemed to be in charge.

Slowly removing my wallet I opened it to reveal my driver's license and held it out for the police officers to see.

"Take it out, please, sir."

I removed my driver's license and carefully handed it to the policeman who looked at it then at me and after assuring himself that I was me handed it back. "Is this your house?"

"No. It belongs to my parents."

"Right then; just what seems to be the problem?"

"When I got home the door was open and it was clear someone had been in here."

"How do you know someone has been in your house and that you didn't leave the door ajar?"

"I always shut and lock the door and everything is a mess inside."

"We'll take a look; c'mon Constable." The officer that had been doing all the talking commanded.

"Sir." His subordinate replied, stepping through the door with his hand at the ready on his weapon.

I Let Tippy out of the car and waited with her on a leash in the backyard for the officers to clear the house. It wasn't long before they emerged reassuring me that the house was now officially declared safe. "Was anything missing?" enquired the man in charge.

"Not that I could tell."

"It was probably just some drug addict looking for drugs or cash. They won't be back.

My name is, Sergeant Mal Content and this is Corporal Lauren Oarder. If you find anything missing call our office and we'll make a report." He said handing me his card.

"Have a good day. Let's go, Corporal." And with that, the officers got back in their car and left.

Mum and Dad returned just as I had begun cleaning up the disarray. I told them what had found when I got home and what the local plods had done and said. Mum offered to clean up but I said, "Thanks, Mum, but I've pretty much got everything under control. I'll leave your bedroom to you. There are just some pictures askew, cushions out of place, doors left open and drawers messed up.

I think I'll order a couple of pizzas for supper. What do you like on yours, Mum?"

"Just cheese, pepperoni and pineapple, please, Justin."

"Dad?"

"The same as your mother."

"Okay; two Hawaiian pizzas."

I picked up the phone and ordered two medium pizzas, one Hawaiian and one all-dressed.

By the time the pizzas arrived, I had the house back in order and had found nothing missing. Whatever the intruder or intruders had been searching for they hadn't found it.

Tippy and I did a perimeter check, locking doors and latching windows and satisfied everything was buttoned up I got ready for bed.

I was just sinking, down into the twilight of blissful slumber where conscious thought dissolves into gently lapping waves of early-stage dreaming when the discordant jangle of the telephone jarred me awake. Mum knocked on my door to tell me that Nack was on the phone and it sounded important. I wrapped my housecoat around me and went to the kitchen. Fumbling with the receiver I groggily said, "Hello."

I heard Nack's rather agitated voice on the other end of the line, "I'm sorry, did I wake you? It's only 9:00 pm.

I analyzed the sample you gave me. Where did you say you found it?"

"It was on the ground in front of Gonnar Keep. Why? What is it?"

"I don't even know if we should be talking about this over the phone. It's a drug called Hyoscine, commonly called Scopolamine. This is very serious, Justin."

"Isn't that what the veterinarian found in the horse in Thelost Village?"

"Ya, it's also known as Devil's Breath and the most dangerous drug in the world."

"What? Wow!" I exclaimed.

"Ya. It's in the class of drugs called anticholinergics that block the neurotransmitter acetylcholine. It's tasteless and odourless and can be administered orally, subcutaneously, ophthalmically, intravenously or transdermally.

It's called the zombie drug because it leaves its victims conscious but without free will. Their mind and actions can be controlled by anyone without leaving a trace of memory."

"We need to tell the police about this. Don't we?" Scenarios were swirling around in my head as I replied, "They wouldn't be very happy if they found out I held some evidence back, especially since the packet they got was empty. Do you have enough left over for them to analyze?"

"Ya, the police need to be told, Justin. I only needed a few grains so there's plenty left for more testing."

"Someone broke in here while we were at Heidi's today. They ransacked the place looking for something. Maybe they were looking for the baggie. We need to decide what to do before someone gets hurt. Let's sleep on it and I'll come to your place to pick up the vile tomorrow."

"Okay, but I won't get any sleep tonight." Nack sounded panicky.

The next morning I was up bright and early having not slept at all well. I had just popped two slices of bread into the toaster when the telephone rang. Picking up the receiver I said, "Hello."

"Justin?" I recognized Lawson's voice and something in it told me this wasn't a social call.

"Hi, Lawson; you're bright and early." I greeted.

"I just got off the phone with Nack and he says Shirley has gone missing," Lawson said seriously.

"Shirley who?"

"Conservation Officer Shirley I. M. Wright. We met her in Allegory Park. Remember?"

"Oh, ya; how does he know she's missing?" I asked Lawson but what I wanted to say but didn't was, 'Was it before or after their first date?'

"Nack said that Hugo's been calling her but she doesn't answer her phone and she didn't show up for their date last night."

"Did Hugo call Conservation Officer Luke A. Bird or the Ministry of Natural Resources?"

"He can't get a hold of Bird and Natural Resources doesn't open until Monday morning. We're meeting at Nack's in an hour do you want me to swing by and pick you up?"

"Sounds good I'll be waiting. I'll fill you in with what's happened to me and what I know when you pick me up."

I could hear Tippy padding down the hall to greet me. "Hi there pal," I said stroking her head and rubbing her silky ears.

Mum sat at the kitchen table drinking her morning coffee.

I said, "Something has happened and I need to meet the guys at Nack's place."

"Do you need anything? Sandwiches, a drink?" she asked.

"Nope; we'll be fine. Thanks, Mum."

It wasn't long before I heard the sounds of tires on gravel. Tippy let out a bark and rushed excitedly to the door to greet whoever our new visitor was. Lawson was climbing out of his truck as I reached the door. Tippy's solid tail beat a tattoo on the wall as she wiggled in anticipation.

I opened the door and she rushed out and jumped up putting her two front paws on his shoulders. "Well hello, Tippy." He said chuckling.

Without wasting any more time I put Tippy back in the house, much to her dismay and Lawson and I got in his truck and headed for Nack's.

Once we were on the road I told Lawson about the break-in, the baggie and the vile containing the dangerous powder that Nack had analyzed. "According to what Nack told me there would have been more than enough chemical left in the baggie for analysis when I turned it over to Bird."

"So, what; you think Bird took what was left in the baggie?"

"I don't know but I can't see who else had the opportunity to replace the baggie I gave him with a clean baggie preventing any trace drugs being found. And he was quick to retrieve the photo evidence and baggie.

Do you remember, Nack saw dried thornapples, in what we had thought was an old abandoned laboratory? And do you remember the smell in that old mine behind the shed?"

"Ya, it smelled like perfume or flowers. Why?"

"Well, the thornapples are the seed pods of the Devil's Trumpet the plant that contains Scopolamine and the scent we detected in the mine is the scent of the Devil's Trumpet."

"So, do you think Bird has gone back to Allegory Park?"

"I'd bet money on it, Lawson."

"Then we better get a move on." Lawson asserted enthusiastically. I knew he was just itching for a brawl.

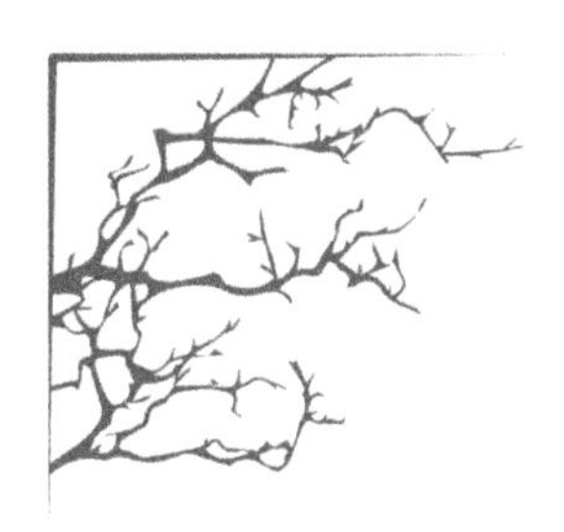

7 Miss Judged

The dull overcast sky suited the grave mood of our band of would-be rescuers. Rain and high winds were forecast but we weren't about to let that stop us.

Nick, Nack, Moose and an anxious Hugo awaited us on Nack's front lawn. The strident din of an alarm could be heard as Lawson and I got out of his truck. Nack instinctively reached for his pager and straight away realized he was on the horns of a dilemma. He was a member of the volunteer firefighters and this was an emergency call to a fire. Now he was torn between honouring his commitment to the community and honouring his commitment to his friend.

Nick saw that his brother was in a predicament so he said, "Nack, let's go put this fire down then we'll catch up with the guys."

Nack looked Hugo in the eye hoping to get his go-ahead and Hugo said, "Ya, Nack. This may be just a wild-goose chase anyway." But he didn't believe that it was. "They need you to fight that fire. Go on. Get a move on. You can catch up later."

Lawson asked Nack, "Can we borrow your canoe? It'll save a lot of time."

"Ya, sure. Me and Nick will get one somewhere on the way, later."

There are those fingernails on the blackboard again as my GPS (Grammatical Pedantry Syndrome) kicked in. 'NICK and I' I screamed in my mind.

"Let's go you guys," Moose said to Lawson, Hugo and me. Snapping me out of my GPS and bringing me back to the urgent task at hand.

We strapped Nack's canoe securely into the back of the truck, climbed in the cab and set out for Allegory Park.

Two hours later found us at the outfitter's picking up a second canoe. We left word that there would be another couple of guys along later for a second canoe.

Reaching the drop-off point at Gravel Lake we eagerly extricated ourselves from the truck, groaning and stretching to get the kinks out. Next, we hauled the canoes out of the back and slid them into the sparkling waters of Gravel Lake, darkened by the gloom of charcoal clouds. We had come prepared with camping gear and rainwear.

Hugo and Moose climbed into Nack's canoe while Lawson and I got into the rental. We began paddling for all we were worth driving our canoes forward until Moose admonished us, "Hey guys. Not only will we not be able to keep up this pace but we won't have anything left in the tank when we get there." We realized he was right and we got into a sustainable rhythm.

When we were out of earshot of the others Lawson said to me, "We should have let the police know what we've found out and where we're going. I should have at least told Billy."

"I called Constable Viola Fuss and explained everything to her. She said that Shirley was an adult and perhaps had decided she no longer wished to go out with Hugo. Then she told me that the conservation officers would deal with it and to not get in the way." I said.

"Sounds like she fobbed you off."

"Yup. That's why I also called Constable Viola Fuss."

"What did she say?"

"She told me not to get involved. She said it was a police matter."

He and I fell silent, each contemplating the wisdom of our mission.

We traversed the familiar route in considerably less time on this occasion and we arrived physically spent but managed to set up camp just as the first of the huge splodges of rain began to fall. Huddled in our tents we tried to relax to recharge our batteries. "Hey, listen. Did you hear something?" I said loud enough for everyone to hear.

We sat motionless listening intently, to the roaring wind and the pelting rain as the storm raged around us, for even the slightest sound of movement. "Was that a growl?" Hugo asked nervously.

"Probably thunder." Responded Lawson as the faint tuneless warble of someone whistling drifted on the wind.

The thudding of footfalls and snapping of twigs could be heard as something unseen crashed through the underbrush. There was a brilliant flash as a massive bolt of lightning lit the lake and surrounding shoreline with the brilliant radiance of a bright sunny day as eerie shadows played fleetingly over our tent walls. All at once the rain stopped and an unnerving silence enveloped us until the air was split with a blood-curdling inhuman scream followed by a mournful wail.

We looked at one another wide-eyed wondering what terrors awaited us on our rescue mission and whether or not we had embarked on a fool's errand. Without further hesitation, Lawson had unzipped our tent door and was halfway out when he spotted something moving out on the lake. As he watched he was happily surprised to see our two bedraggled and battered friends approaching the shore. "Well, I don't believe it! Look who's here!" he shouted to the rest of us as I scrambled after him, Hugo and Moose weren't far behind. After a hearty greeting, Nack explained, "It was an old empty house and was fully engaged when we got there. We had it under control in twenty minutes, so, we weren't far behind you guys."

"Ya, we managed to save the basement." Nick added with a wink and chuckle."

Our night terrors of the howling beast thrashing about in the woods around us were soon forgotten.

Nick and Nack changed into dry clothes and were ready to face our next challenge.

Lawson, always a man of action, was already on the move calling over his shoulder as he entered the forest, "Pitter patter let's get at 'er we're burning daylight."

We followed the path that led to the mine and then to Gonnar Keep. "Where do you think they're keeping her?" whispered Hugo.

"I don't know but let's check out the mine first. It's on our way," replied Lawson.

The cold, sodden underbrush soaked our pant legs and it was difficult to keep our footing as we rushed along the slimy mud of the pathway trying to be as quiet as possible lest we alert the kidnappers to our presence.

Arriving at the mine site Lawson came to an abrupt halt. There was movement in the darkness of the shed that concealed the entrance to the mine. We waited and watched as two burly thugs in hoodies. *Did you ever notice that only villains, chancers and wrong 'uns wear hoodies?* backed out of the doorway uncoiling some sort of cable or wire from a spool.

Lawson was the first to recognize the significance. "They're going to blow up the mine. We have to stop them." He whispered in surprise.

Just as Lawson charged toward the men Hugo reached into his pocket and withdrew two polished white spheres. With lightning speed he drew back his arm and with the aim of a skilled marksman hurled one of the dimpled balls with deadly accuracy and force, narrowly missing the back of Lawson's head. The glossy missile caught the closest criminal behind the ear and he instantly went face down like a giant redwood being felled. He reloaded and cocked his arm back but before he could release his missile Lawson reached the remaining and very startled miscreant. The element of surprise gave Lawson the opportunity he needed. He delivered a powerful right hook to the jaw of the would-be demolition man. We could hear a sound like dry twigs cracking as his jawbone shattered rendering him unconscious. He landed like a big sack of potatoes on the ground beside his partner in crime. Fortunately, they had not had time to activate the detonating device which lay precariously in the hoodlum's outstretched hand.

A wide, satisfied grin spread across Lawson's face.

I knelt down and gingerly took the detonator from the unconscious hood's dangerously twitching hand; his finger still poised on the button. Quickly and carefully I disconnected the blasting wires. I smashed the detonator while Moose and Nack ran into the mine to disconnect the wires from the explosives. They traced the wires to a large number of explosives planted strategically just outside the big steel door that remained closed and locked.

While Nack, Hugo and Moose set to work tying the thugs' feet and hands then securing them each in the shade of a tree with the blasting cables Lawson and I dashed into the tunnel. Nick followed us into the mine and grabbed up a pick axe as he ran through the shed. Lawson indicated the lock to Nick who knew immediately what to do and with a single well-placed blow he shattered the lock. Lawson and I tugged on the door which seemed immovable at first but almost imperceptibly a sliver of light could be seen around the edges. The ancient hinges made grating, creaking sounds of protest as the door began its agonizingly slow progress. The sliver widened little by little, until at last, the door was wide enough to get our first glimpse of what lay beyond the portal. It was nightmarish. Many of the enslaved mindlessly continued to perform their assigned tasks while others milled about aimlessly like zombies in a scene from Night of the Living Dead. A few seemed startled and confused by our sudden and unexpected appearance.

Disturbingly two colonists lay amid piles of soggy detritus silent and unmoving as though lifeless. Nack rushed ahead of us to check the vitals of the two apparent corpses. Grasping the wrist of the closest one Nack was taken aback when suddenly their eyes fluttered. Then to our astonishment, the two seemingly deceased were reanimated rising and returning to their tasks like automatons.

"It's the scopolamine." Nack explained to us.

Lawson shouted, "We're here to help. We need to get everyone out of here as quickly as possible." And with that, we set to work trying to revive those we could and direct everyone to the exit and safety.

The few that were lucid began helping those that weren't. Women wept as they clutched their children and men shook our hands as they filed past us. Suddenly a petite and very pretty blond woman wrapped her arms around Nick hugging him as if she'd never let go. Finally, she released her hold and stepped back embarrassed; quietly apologizing for being too forward as tears trickled down her cheeks, "I'm very sorry for my familiarity, sir. I was simply overwhelmed with gratitude. Do you not remember me?"

It was at that moment that recognition dawned on Nick as he went red in the face stammering, "H...how could I forget you? Y... you brought cold water to my job site. We... we're just glad to find you alive. Are you alright? My name is Nick." He paused hoping she would give him her name.

"Th... Thank you for rescuing me... uh... I mean us sir... er... I mean, Nick. My name is Frieda Gogh."

"M...maybe I could come to see you when this is all over?" Nick said questioningly.

She looked up at him with big, smoky blue eyes smiling and nodded timidly. "I'd like that."

"Come along now, Frieda. We mustn't keep these men standing around." The last man through the door chided. Thanking us profusely he introduced himself as, Zeke Himphurst, explaining that he was a village elder and had been powerless against the evil spell cast by the Wendigo. They had been taken from their home, Thelost Village, against their will.

After gathering the villagers together in the clearing Nick instructed Zeke to keep his flock together and watch over their two would-be assassins until the police arrived. We headed for Gonnar Keep with Lawson eagerly leading the way.

Drawing close to the Keep we could hear an irate woman's voice, "Please know that I still maintain a high level of respect for you as my mentor and I thank you sincerely for your support and guidance. I have been proud to work under you.

You will be delighted to know it was your unparalleled instruction that has afforded me the incentive to move forward to new and exciting opportunities as a pirate and purveyor of pharmaceuticals.

Once my crew of unabashed rogues is assembled, we shall take to the capacious expanse of civilization in pursuit of affluence and infamy.

I'm taking applications for First Officer if you're interested. Oh, that's right you'll be dead." She finished laughing sardonically.

Somewhere unseen we could hear the faint sound of someone whimpering and pleading, "Please, Officer Wright... Shirley, think of what you're doing. This is madness. Please, Shirley, don't do this."

"I'm sorry. I was listening until, out of nowhere, I became distracted by this loud, obnoxious noise that turned out to be, YOUR VOICE. I'm **really** going to miss doing all **your** work for you, your disgusting innuendo, and your roaming hands." The woman speaking was hidden from view.

Kneeling in the dense underbrush with a shed between us and the Keep we watched the hive of activity. "I think I heard Shirley's voice. I hope they haven't hurt her. We've got to get her out of there." said an anxious Hugo in hushed tones.

On the porch sat a white-haired old crone who could be seen brandishing her cane in the air from time to time and remonstrating while an extremely brawny middle-aged man and tough-looking woman transported small aluminum containers from the cabin to the backs of waiting four-wheelers. A shotgun leaned menacingly against the wall next to the aged battleaxe.

"What do we do now? They're going to be leaving soon." asked an anxious Hugo.

Moose, ever the tactician, sniffed, raised the corner of his upper lip, adjusted his glasses and said, "Lawson, you and Hugo sneak around behind the cabin to the other side. Their backs are to that side most of the time. Justin, you go around this shed and get ready to grab that shotgun.

I'll watch for our first opportunity then create a diversion and when I do you all attack."

Lawson was already on the move with Hugo matching him step for step as they made their way covertly around the perimeter. Hugo signalled Moose that they were in place. Justin too had circled the shed and awaited Moose's distraction.

"They better not have harmed her. We've got to get her out of there, now." insisted Hugo.

"Well, this is the last of the boxes." a middle-aged Goliath called from the bottom of the stairs to the disembodied voice that had come from inside the cabin.

"One last piece of unfinished business, Pop." A woman's voice called from within the cabin.

Moose chose that moment to step out from his hiding place and start to walk towards the dangerous-looking couple standing at the foot of the stairs. "Hello there. Have you seen my dog?" he asked innocently trying to appear lost and confused.

All eyes were on Moose as he strode nonchalantly toward the incredulous pair.

Immediately, Hugo let fly his last golf ball. Hurtling like a speeding bullet with deadly accuracy it found its target, catching the woman in the centre of her forehead instantly rendering her unconscious.

I had positioned myself crouching just behind the old hag and as she turned to see what moron had the gall to enter their lair I rose stepping first onto a conveniently placed rock and then onto the porch and of all the boards on the deck, of course, I found the loose one. Flipping up it caught me square in the nose momentarily stunning me as tiny dazzling stars twinkled before my eyes. This was going to leave a mark.

Hearing the commotion she turned and just as my fingers wrapped around the barrel of the double-barreled 12 gauge shotgun she took hold of the stock. Her grip was surprisingly strong as she wrenched with all her pint-sized might but I held tight. She struggled to reach the triggers and just as I hoisted the weapon, lifting the clinging crone from her chair, her dangling feet kicked the air furiously as her finger found the triggers. She pulled both simultaneously discharging the weapon indiscriminately. The recoil from the powerful blast caused the hardwood stock of the firearm to slam into her chest with the force of a mule kick, knocking the wind out of her. Her deceivingly wiry little body collapsed in a heap on the porch gasping for air.

Meanwhile, Lawson had leaped into action. He was enjoying himself, grinning from ear to ear as he lowered his head and charged headlong into the overfull breadbasket of the hulking hood. There was a loud oomph as all the air rushed from the lungs of the big man. Lawson buried his shoulder into the solar plexus of the goon folding the six-foot-six combatant in half. Before his opponent could recover Lawson let fly with a fist of iron to the giant's jaw snapping his head around and then he straightened him up with a pile driver uppercut. A silly look came over the miscreant's face as his eyes rolled back in his head and then closed as he went down in a heap like the proverbial sack of potatoes.

There wasn't time for celebration because just then we saw Hugo backing out of the front door of the Keep with his hands raised. "Sorry, Hugo, I was starting to like you but needs must, as they say. Get down there with the others." Shirley ordered.

Hugo turned and dejectedly descended the stairs to join us, all but Moose who seemed to have disappeared.

It's funny the things you never notice ordinarily that become glaringly obvious when you're in the heat of battle. I couldn't help but notice that Shirley had her hair in a bun held in place by a pair of very sharp and lethal-looking hair chopsticks.

It was then she noticed the three prone bodies, "What have you done to my family?" she shrieked hysterically as she waved a sawed-off shotgun in the air indiscriminately.

Framed in the darkened doorway behind his friend's maniacal captor emerged an unlikely hero, so thin he barely cast a shadow. Stepping warily onto the veranda his foot fell upon the one board that would give him away. The slight creek of the board was enough to alert the gun-wielding villain. She was only able to manage a half turn before Moose was upon her desperately grappling for control of the weapon. Like a bolt of lightning, Hugo was up the three steps in a single bound and relieved his ignominious other of her implement of destruction before she could inflict any damage. "I'll take that." He said irritably.

She lashed out violently catching Hugo off guard with a surprisingly successful knee which dropped Hugo to the floor. Like a coiled spring, Moose attacked. His fist caught her in the throat sending her reeling, choking and unable to draw a breath.

A few moments later the thrumming sound of a helicopter could be heard overhead. Next, several heavily armed men clad in black dropped from the sky on ropes and burst from the surrounding forest shouting "POLICE!" and "GET ON THE GROUND, FACE DOWN! HANDS BEHIND YOUR HEADS! NOW! DO IT!"

Face down next to Lawson I whispered, "Isn't it wonderful to live in a society where pizza can get to your house before the police."

Within moments the team leader of the Tactics and Rescue Unit or TRU was satisfied that all was under control. He looked at us, thumbs tucked in his belt, awaiting an explanation.

It was then that a familiar face, Constable Viola Fuss, emerged from the woods. After she vouched for us and we were separated from the villains, our handcuffs were removed.

I briefly explained our presence to an incredulous Team Leader.

"We've got a float plane and helicopter standing by on Goodbye Lake to take you out of here," said Fuss. "The prisoners will be transported first."

"We've got canoes and camping equipment here. If it's all the same we'll stay the night and head back in the morning?"

Addressing the Team Leader I warned, "Be careful of that woman." I said pointing to a trussed-up Shirley. "Those chopsticks holding her hair in place are lethal weapons and I think you might find that one of them was responsible for the death of an RCMP officer."

"Constable."

"Sir?"

"Remove those deadly hair pins and bag them as evidence."

One of the officers was about to open one of the aluminum boxes when Moose yelled, "STOP! Those boxes contain Devil's Breath and any contact will kill you."

A distressed wail was heard from the cabin. The police looked at us for an explanation. Hugo said, "Oh ya. I forgot about him. That's Conservation Officer Luke A. Bird." The TRU team leader nodded to one of his men who cautiously disappeared into the Keep with his weapon at the ready. A few minutes later Bird appeared in the doorway escorted by the officer.

"Who are you?" demanded the team leader.

"Conservation Officer Luke A. Bird. That crazy woman" he said pointing at Shirley, "kidnapped me. She was going to kill me. She's insane I tell you, INSANE!" He bleated hysterically.

"Let's get the miscreants back to the detachment. Tomorrow will be time enough for your debriefing." He said.

Heaving a collective sigh of relief my band of brothers from other mothers and I headed back to camp. Upon our return, we witnessed the last of the villagers being loaded into the float plane for transport home where they would undergo thorough medical examinations.

The adrenaline was wearing off giving rise to profound fatigue and a peculiar excruciating throbbing in my face. Raising my hand to my nose it was then I remembered stepping on the loose plank of wood and it unceremoniously coming up to meet me.

Nick was looking dejected as he watched the villagers climb aboard the plane. That is until he heard a tender voice behind him, "Nick."

Turning he was elated to find Frieda. "I couldn't leave until I knew you were alright."

Nick walked her to the waiting plane and saw her safely aboard.

8 DEATH POINTS HIS FINGER

Be sober, be vigilant: because your adversary, the devil, as a roaring lion, walketh about seeking whom he may devour. 1 Peter 5:8 KJV

A week had passed. Statements had been taken and cell doors had clanked shut on I. M. Shirley Wright and her family. It was Friday night and Heidi had invited us all to a barbeque.

She took one look at me and exclaimed, "What happened to your face?"

The swelling had gone down considerably but the bruising around my eyes made me look like a raccoon. "You should see the other guy." I quipped.

"Does it still hurt?"

"That'll teach him to pick on defenceless little old ladies." Hugo taunted.

"It looks worse than it is. At least it wasn't broken." I said.

"Did you ever find out who all those people were?" she asked.

"Conservation Officer Luke A. Bird told us the legend about Gonnar Dayz, the uranium miner, and his missing daughter, I. M. Ina Dayz?" I said.

"Ya, what did she have to do with all of this? She's got to have been dead for years?" asked Nick doubtfully.

"She was never lost. She ran off with her cousin, Sunny. They had a daughter, Eileen. Eileen Dayz married Hugh B. Wright and they had a daughter, I. M. Shirley Wright.

I. M. Ina Dayz isn't dead. That belligerent old bat on the veranda with the shotgun was Ina. She rules the family with an iron fist.

She wanted what she believed was her property. Over the years the family had tried to regain control of Gonnar Keep and the land but could never prove a legitimate claim to the title.

Constable Fuss told me that every member of the family has a rap sheet as long as your arm. Mostly petty crime but they've managed to keep Shirley clean because Ina had a plan. They would use their ancestral estate to hatch a scheme that would not only make them rich but hit back at the authorities in a major way." I paused.

Moose looked perplexed as he asked, "Wait, where have I heard that name? What was it, oh ya, Eileen something."

"Eileen Wright. She was the disdainful clerk at the Prince Edward County Registry Office. I'm sure her family operated the drug lab at 1758 Sleepy Hollow Lane and I'm equally certain she called them at the lab to warn them I was on my way. That's when they changed the sign and property numbers. But that's just speculation and I have no definitive evidence but it fits."

"Hey Justin, what happened to the baggie you were going to give to the police? The one with the white powder?" asked Nack.

"I made copies of the photos after our pool game to turn over to the OPP along with the baggie the next morning but Conservation Officer Luke A. Bird showed up at my house that night and said he'd deliver the pictures and the baggie to the police. I found out from Constable Viola Fuss that Shirley admitted to meeting Bird and offering to take the evidence to the police forensics. That's when she switched the baggie containing the remnants of the drug for a clean baggie."

"Well, don't leave us hanging. What was her plan?" asked Nick.

"Hugh and Eileen had been involved in small-time drug dealing and trafficking and had heard about the perfect substance for an easy crime, Devil's Trumpet or Jimsonweed. It is easily grown in moist, fertile, well-drained soil and does not attract the attention of the police." I carried on.

Moose arched his upper lip, sniffed deeply, adjusted his glasses and interjected, "Scopolamine or Devil's Breath is a fine white powder made by crushing the seeds of the plant. Pre-Colombian South American shamans took their mind-altering drugs very seriously. A pouch containing remnants of at least five psychotropic drugs, from at least three different plants, has been found in a bundle thought to be used in a shamanic ritual, indicating the thought put into preparing for these events a millennia ago.

It is tasteless and odourless and can be administered orally, ophthalmically, intravenously or topically; eliminating, completely, free will, leaving the victim conscious but with their actions in absolute control of the predator, with no memory afterwards. This makes it ideal for corrupt use. It has been used by Josef

Mengele as a truth serum, the CIA in behavioural engineering experiments and Colombian criminals use it in many criminal activities."

I persisted, "In fact, when the police searched the mine that the two hoods were getting set to blow up they discovered an aerosol system used to covertly for mass distribution of Devil's Breath. This kept every last one of the kidnapped residents of Thelost Village, including women and children, in a continual zombie state. They continued tending the plants with no idea that their greenhouse prison was about to be destroyed with them in it."

"Ya, ya, that's all very interesting but what was her plan?" interrupted an impatient Nick.

"Constable Fuss told me that Shirley has been diagnosed as a... Let's see here. I wrote it down." I unfolded the paper I had written it on. "Right, 'she's a psychopath exhibiting strong antisocial, aggressive, perverted, criminal and amoral tendencies without empathy or remorse'." I read.

I went on, "Between Ina's ruthless determination and Shirley's psychopathy they initially planned to get their family property back and punish those they felt stole it. However, the psychiatrist was certain that Shirley's insatiability would drive her to ever greater acts of evil." I concluded.

"Did the police ever find out who the zombie was they caught at The Last Resort in Allegory Park or how he died?" asked Moose.

Irrationally I uneasily lowered my voice as if I might be overheard and said, "Constable Viola Fuss told me that the doctor could not find a definitive cause of death. Blood tests showed high levels of Devil's Breath. His body has mysteriously vanished. To this day they've never found his body but the RCMP think he was one of their undercover narcotics agents that has gone missing, code-named, WENDIGO."

I looked over at Notcho sprawled on the grass beside Heidi's chair looking very contented. She stirred raising her head as if something only she had become aware of caught her attention. She was on alert. I watched as her ears cocked towards the house and an open window. Sniffing the air and listening intently she began to move toward the house.

I got up, "You want to go in so you can come out?" I asked her and climbing the steps opened the door for her.

She gave me a look that seemed to say, "Don't you hear that? Someone's calling me."

Looking inside I noticed the cellar door stood open. This time I heard the faint hoarse whisper, "Notcho, come." Curious, I followed her to the door. She started down the stairs just as something moved in the darkness. It was the sound of beating wings. It was only that pesky raven.

Then she caught a whiff of something interesting amid a plethora of scents and following her nose descended the rest of the steps. "Over here, you mangy cur." came the voice from the shadows. Then she came upon it. It was mostly buried. She thought her mistress would want to know about her discovery. She felt sorry for it and was sure the extended member she helped herself to would not be missed by its owner. "In fact," she thought, "its owner would, in a manner of speaking be pointing the way to its undisclosed and ghastly eternal internment".

Still standing at the cellar door Notcho ascended the staircase with her prize and as she passed me I reached down to take it. "Whatcha got there, Notcho?" I asked. Turning her head to avoid me she marched past and went straight outside to Heidi.

Just then Heidi felt a wet nose gently touch her arm and looking down saw Notcho's dirt-covered face with a look of self-satisfaction. Notcho looked Heidi in the eye and appeared to say, "I have found something very important. We need to get help." As she stroked her silky head Notcho deposited her offering in the palm of her mistress' outstretched hand.

"You've been digging in the cellar again, haven't you?" Heidi admonished her four-legged companion.

Holding her hand in the light from their bonfire she was taken aback to discover the gruesome gift was a badly decomposed human finger. It was then she realized Notcho had given her the finger. Shrieking she dropped the digit which landed in the bonfire coals.

"Where'd that come from?" I asked reaching furiously to free the phalange from the fire.

"I'm not sure; perhaps the cellar. She seems curious about what's down there. I bet she's been digging in the cellar." said Heidi.

We all rushed into the house and made our way down into the cellar with Notcho eagerly leading the way. The dim light from the single incandescent bulb dangling from the ceiling illuminated Notcho standing proudly over a freshly dug hole. What appeared to be a skeletal hand seemed to be reaching out from its earthen place of repose.

"We must not disturb this area any further. I'll call DSS Kaye right now!" I said. Upstairs I dialled the police department number and after what seemed an eternity a perpetually pooped O'Kaye picked up. "What is it this time, Mr. Case?"

"I think we may have found the final resting place of Longue John Silver III," I said into the telephone.

There was silence on the other end of the line then, "We'll be right there. Don't touch a thing."

It wasn't long before Heidi's home was once again overrun by police and forensics.

It was a restless weekend for everyone. Monday afternoon Heidi received a visit from DSS Kaye. "I regret to inform you, Miss Jewels, that the remains found in your basement have been positively identified as those of Longue John Silver III."

"Oh, how awful1 How did he die and was it quick?"

"Mr. Silver was struck on the head with a bronze statue that was, in fact, part of the original inventory of Mr. Silver and found in Mr. Dewey's possession. The Medical Examiner assures me death would have been almost instantaneous."

"Why didn't the killer dump his body in the lake?"

"It is our assumption, that he didn't want it to be found washed up on a beach. The inexplicably massive head wound would have led to a presumption of murder and a search for the murderer."

"Was Mr. Dewey the murderer?"

"Autopsy matched the bronze statue to the wound found in the back of Mr. Silver's skull. Forensics was able to pull three usable prints from the statue matching those of Mr. Hugh Louis Dewey of Dewey, Cheetham & Howe, LLB.

Undoubtedly, he died at the hand of Mr. Dewey. He has been formally charged with murder."

Again, I'm sorry for your loss Miss Jewels." He offered as he turned to leave.

"Thank you, DSS Kaye." She said as he turned to leave.

A single deep guttural croak was heard as if demanding attention. Looking up Heidi and DSS Kaye observed a huge midnight black harbinger perched high atop the old house. "Wendigo" Was all that the raven said.

9 Wendigos Walk Among Us

I contemplated the contrast of modern horror stories that appropriate the wendigo as a plot device to what actually ought to be terrifying to us, that we live in societies enveloped in violence and exploitation that we struggle to identify as such. What if the monstrosity we face is in fact, not an otherworldly presence but our all too human selves?

There are those living among us infected by a corrosive drive toward self-aggrandizing greed and excessive consumption, traits that sow disharmony and destruction. Agents of social cannibalism who know no restrictions, expressing the darkest aspects of human nature; these are the WENDIGOS that walk among us. It will be the person you least suspect, the person standing next to you in line, or perhaps someone you know.

Are you a Wendigo?

"Evil grows in the dark
where the sun it never shines.
It grows in cracks and holes
and lives in people's minds[4]"

Remember you can have everything in life you want if you will just help enough other people get what they want.

ABOUT THE AUTHOR

I was born an "only child" but a funny thing happened in grade 7. I acquired brothers! Yup, 7 of them!

---

[1] **Ameliasburgh** is named after Princess Amelia, the 15th child of King George III.

[2] Based on "A Barrel of Gold" by C. H. Widdifield found in "Picturesque Prince Edward County" by Helen M. Merrill 1892

[3] Wikipedia: A goniometry meters an instrument that either measures an angle or allows an object to be rotated to a precise angular position. In crystallography, goniometry meters are used for measuring angles between crystal faces.

[4] Lyrics written by Terry Jacks and sung by The Poppy Family

Don't miss out!

Visit the website below and you can sign up to receive emails whenever James D. A. Terry publishes a new book. There's no charge and no obligation.

https://books2read.com/r/B-A-KFBH-NAENC

Connecting independent readers to independent writers.

About the Author

Upon retirement from international finance James D. A. Terry embarked on a new journey into the esoteric and always interesting realm of the mystery adventure writer.

James lives in Ontario, Canada and enjoys reading, writing and travel.

The Curious Case of the Vanishing Victims, his first novel under his own name, is a fictional reminiscence of Justin Case, Termination Agent for the Tin Can Communications Company, set in the 1970s.

Disguised as the enigmatic and man of mystery, Solomon Knight, whose very raison d'être is to squeeze every last delicious drop out of life and always in search of adventure penned four books in a series about a 20th century International League of Paladins.

Evil Lurks in the Dark, the first in a series about modern day international paladins, is a book overflowing with mystery and action. Learn the origins of the International League of Paladins and their raison d'etre. Solve the riddle of the Ghost of Greyman Cottage; Plumb the depths to get to the bottom of the deep dark Secret at Sinister Lake; Death will point its bony finger at a murderer in Coffinsrise; and last but certainly not least, join our intrepid adventurers in the quest for the secret to the Philosopher's Stone.

Read more at https://readingroombyjames.wixsite.com/author.

Milton Keynes UK
Ingram Content Group UK Ltd.
UKHW020750151223
434437UK00019B/955